AN
ISLAND
HEART

AN ISLAND HEART

A NOVEL

BRIAN O'ROURKE

Wynkin deWorde

2 0 0 5

Published in 2005
by

Wynkin deWorde

Wynkin deWorde Ltd.,
PO Box 257, Galway, Ireland.
info@deworde.com

A CIP catalogue record for this book is available from the British Library

ISBN: 1-904893-07-4

Typesetting: Patricia Hope, Skerries, Co. Dublin, Ireland
Executive Editor: Valerie Shortland
Cover Design: Roger Derham
Cover Design Coordination: Design Direct, Galway, Ireland
Printed by Betaprint, Dublin, Ireland

for
Paula Carroll

"O, if I was given
to tail – baring,
I have my own
secrets to discover."

–Winifred Jenkins,
in Tobias Smollett,

The Expedition of Humphry Clinker

04 04 04

My children – Seán, Humphrey, Iseult, Terry, Hamlet, Eve, Adam, Leo, Seamus,

I have often wondered what it feels like to have your mother murdered by your father. I'll never know, of course, but you soon will.

Jealousy? Au contraire: *sexual harrassment over seventeen, eighteen years. (By her, that is, by her.)*

After a fortnight's haring around, I had decided to go back on some of my tablets and to immerse myself for the weekend in a theological critique of Darwinism – Desde el mono hasta el hombre: paso imposible, *by one Ildefonso de Remolacha y Cataplón. I was still savouring the title page when she entered the study, wearing her Mona Lisa look, and informed me – reminded me, she claimed – that she had arranged an 'interesting' weekend for us in the cottage. I said what I always say – said – but as she swanned out, humming, I was all Krakatoa inside. And then I heard a voice: 'It's time to put a Desde to her Mona.' And simultaneously I saw, I witnessed the scene we just recently enacted. I was the one humming on the way here.*

1

She expired unresisting, in high pleasure, assuming, I presume, that I was cranking her up a couple of notches more.

The question is not: 'Is Hamlet mad?', but: 'Is Othello mad?' As sane as myself, I say.

When, eventually, I lifted the pillow off her face, I was astounded: she was 21 again, more beautiful than the first time, and more serene than anyone I've ever seen. 'She knows,' *the voice said,* 'the dead know.'

I'm not saying that there's an afterlife. Or that there isn't. But there's a nowlife. There's a heaven, and I'm in it: a calm, ecstatic understanding of, well, everything. I was here once before, twelve years ago to the day. If it's a foretaste, well and good. If it's all there is, it makes having lived worthwhile.

I met the Prophet a few days ago, walking near Poul. 'Woe to you, Enda Ring!' he thundered. 'All you can think about is women's bottoms, when you could be navigating the unfathomable God.' From where I'm sitting, the journey from the one to the other seems not impossible.

You wouldn't believe the tenderness I feel towards your mother at this moment.

It's strange, writing this. I don't know you, I feel no bond with a single one of you. You weren't my idea.

'What kind of man is he?' . . . am I? The attached pages – I carry them everywhere – provide a clue. They contain stories I wrote during my 1995 'episode'. They are in essence autobiographical, the covering letters more nakedly so. I have arranged them in a sequence which is not that of their composition: in my attempts at self-discovery I fell under the spell of the mirror.

What will I do now? I'll throw on some clothes and wait. And see. Oh yes, I'll see. Of that I'm certain; for some time at least, I'll see.

Your father

PRINCE

Excellency,

(Or should I have written 'Dear Salina'?; 'Dear Don Fabrizio'?; 'Dear Prince'?), I address you with a certain trepidation, knowing your capacity for irony and anger. Let me say too, though, that I delight in some of your one-liners: ' . . . seven children I've had with her, seven; and never once have I seen her navel'. 'Love. Of course, love. Flames for a year, ashes for thirty'. 'How could one inveigh against those sure to die?'. And I suppose what I like most about you is your doubleness. Your strong fingers, to give one example, could bend spoons and coins, but they were equally adept at manipulating the delicate mechanism of a telescope, and at stroking the flesh of your wife or of a Palermo whore. You confessed weekly to a chaplain, and you had a sense of sin, but your heaven was in the serenity of the stars, and you envisaged your death as a tryst with Venus. You were a pagan, in a word, but a Sicilian Catholic pagan. I rejoiced in your paganism from the time I first read The Leopard, but there was one incident, which pulled me up short, and still does. You were on your way to a ball with the ladies of your family. A tinkling bell announced the passage of a priest bearing the Blessed Sacrament to an invalid. The ladies crossed themselves, but you got out of the

5

carriage and knelt on the pavement. That shook me. And it brought back an episode that had upended me.

I had met a delightful young woman named Louise and was tentatively exploring possibilities. We walked through the streets of Galway one Thursday afternoon, risking the odd touch, indulging in the kind of banter that goes with such situations. At a children's playground we sat on the swings and careered down the slide. Suddenly there was the sound of hymn-singing, and a tiny Corpus Christi procession passed. I stood and stared, oblivious to Louise; I was back in my childhood, but also overcome by embarrassment. The idea of kneeling never occurred to me. I followed the procession with my eyes, and was astounded to see Louise walk briskly after it and join its ranks. Looking down beside me I saw the print of her two knees in the sand. A couple of days later I received a note saying she was not interested in a relationship with a pagan. I was well rid of her, perhaps, but I was very much attracted to her too. Once more I was sore for a spell.

Allow me to tell you a story, one of the many that well up in me as ceaselessly as sea-waves, and that threaten to drag me under, or bear me towards the shore, I can' t tell which.

My name is Cora Stone. I'm from Dublin and I'm 24. Everything that matters has happened to me in the past two years – since I went to Paris to do a Master's. I was practically a virgin then – there had been one drunken one-night stand the year before – and I had notions of romance as well as of more laid-back study.

And I did find romance, and very quickly: in a swimming pool. The place did not surprise me – I'd spent most of my leisure time since childhood in such surroundings; what amazed me was the kind of man I fell for: Jean-Christophe, besides being tall, dark and handsome, was secretary of the Paris Guild of Catholic Philosophy Students. I'd never met anyone so attentive, good-humoured or charming, and the evenings we spent together were delightful. There were no nights together – that wouldn't have been his philosophy – but I found I didn't mind overmuch: the rest made up. We laughed a lot: in particular I remember a night when Jean-Christophe tickled me and I tried to teach him a verse that Daddy used to repeat while tickling me (even when Mummy thought me too old for tickles):

Up the airy mountain,
Down the rushy glen,
We daren't go a-hunting
For fear of little men;
Wee folk, good folk,
Trooping all together;
Green jacket, red cap,
And white owl's feather.

His English was pretty limited. On one occasion, as we played in the pool, he called me "*mon petit phoque*". '*Phoque*' is a seal; he had no idea it could suggest anything else, and I couldn't bring myself to explain the joke. Something else happened shortly afterwards which proved the strength of the spell I was under: as we arrived at the pool, he gently took my bikini from me and handed me a one-piece swimsuit;

"This will look much better on you," he said, and I put up no resistance.

I was introduced to his parents, and invited back; I visited a few times. His father, like Daddy, was a doctor, and his mother had a brother a bishop. I was made to feel part of the family. And my own parents – rarely unanimous – gave me their blessing, on the phone and when I came home for Christmas.

Shortly after I returned to Paris, Jean-Christophe brought me to an Irish pub called The Thatch. Since it was the feast of the Epiphany, he said, he wished to declare himself and show forth the desires of his heart: would I marry him? I would. He placed a string of pearls around my neck and took the rest of my breath with a kiss; the centre pearl was the biggest I'd ever seen.

I wore the necklace every day: it was a ring of protective

magic, enclosing me in a troublefree world. I floated gently, lapped and lulled in a delicious dreamy doze.

On the first of February I awoke. I was back in The Thatch on my own: Jean-Christophe was at a meeting. I was there to hear a piper form Cork named Finny Fisher; the name was new to me. I sat just in front of the little stage, and my first glimpse of him brought a frisson, like a dive into a rock pool at dawn. He was of medium height, and thin; he had longish, jet-black hair, and his beard was clipped short and dusted with grey. His eyes were cold and intense, and I suspected that piping did precious little to exhaust his energies. He played, with minimum commentary, and I was mesmerised. Looking up, I saw him as a figure on the prow of a ship, powering the ship forward with his force. And I was in the sea below him, borne forward by the swell he generated. When I focused on his pipes, I became fascinated especially by the bag, hypnotised by the movement of his elbow. I fancied that I *was* the bag, or was *in* it, clothed in it. And sometimes the two illusions fused, and I was riding the waves, wearing the bag like a skin.

During the interval I sat in a daze, but at the end I approached and introduced myself. I asked him where he was going next, and he listed a few places in Brittany. I heard myself saying: "I want to go with you." He looked at me a second, then said, "OK."

I took off my necklace and gave it to the barman, with a note telling Jean-Christophe I was returning to Ireland; I knew he would enquire for me in The Thatch very soon. Then I went with Finny to his hotel, where he judged me the finest set of pipes he'd ever played. I was charmed, and took to christening our bouts of love with the names of tunes. "The Bucks of Oranmore," I gasped, as he approached a climax; but it fell to him to exclaim "Foxhunters!" when I yelped like an animal attacked. We surfaced around ten; I went to my place and packed my bags, and in the afternoon we boarded a bus for Brest.

The next fortnight was fairytale: walks, talks, music, wine, love . . . Whether listening to or substituting for Finny's pipes, I was moving in my own true medium. At his gigs I hauled in dazzling catches with my tape-recorder – the latest model, Daddy's Christmas gift. I watched his fans flock round him like seagulls: I saw '*The Rambling Mermaid*' – his tape and CD – take flight . . . When the tour ended we sailed to Cork and settled in Finny's flat on French's Quay. Within days I was earning money from translations, and becoming accustomed to bliss.

My parents were not impressed. They were united in shock and bewilderment when I announced my return by phone; they were appalled when I informed them about Finny. I visited at Easter. Mummy ranted about family and self-respect and living in sin and hippies drawing the dole. Daddy, with a hand on her arm and his eyes fixed on mine, said, "It will blow over, dear; Cora will come to her senses."

"That's precisely what I have done," I told him, "and I recommend the life of the senses." It was a brief visit.

I kept contact to a minimum after that, and immersed myself in my new life. But their twenty-fifth anniversary was coming up, and I decided to travel home on the day before. I got to the house around six; there was no sign of life. I let myself in, and found a letter from Jean-Christophe inside the door. It informed me that he had suffered, that he did not understand, that he respected my freedom, and that he forgave me. His ordeal had paved the way for the decision he had just taken: to be a priest. He would enter a seminary in the autumn, and the memory of my goodness would remain an inspiration. I ran a hot bath and lay for ages, imagining Jean-Christophe as my confessor: '*Oui, mon petit phoque . . .*' – as I teased him with accounts of my music-making.

When I emerged, I realised I had no towel, so I headed for the hot press. As I passed my parents' bedroom, the door opened and my mother emerged in her night-gown. She was instantly berserk.

"You slut!" she shrieked, "You Jezebel! Your lady-killer isn't enough for you, you have to try to tempt your father too!"

And she lashed out with the nearest thing to hand, a hairdryer. I'd seen fits like this before. I grasped her by the wrists, pushed her into the room, heaved her on to the bed, threw the duvet over her, straddled her, and pressed her face into the pillows. When she stopped struggling I relaxed. She didn't move. She wasn't breathing.

My mind whirled; I saw courtroom scenes. Then I grabbed the hairdryer, and attacked the wet parts of the duvet, my teeth chattering. I wasn't halfway through when Daddy walked in.

"What's going on?" he asked.

"She's dead," I answered.

He checked. I told him what had happened. He stared at me throughout my recital. "Go and get dressed," he said then.

The post-mortem said cardiac arrest, nothing about asphyxiation. I had a breakdown anyway. I was a month in hospital, drugged. I phoned a friend of Finny's, it seems, and Finny himself came to see me. I don't remember his visit; I sat combing my hair, I heard later, all the time that he talked.

When I was discharged, I wrote saying I wasn't ready to go back to him yet. He understood. I sat at home as summer died into autumn, reading Dostoevsky –*Crime and Punishment, The Idiot, The Brothers Karamazov.* I enjoyed none of it, understood little, and remembered next to nothing, but it kept my mind from gnawing at itself. Daddy was attentive and gentle. Slowly, imperceptibly, the gloom lifted. I began to think about Cork, but at the same time, for the first time, I found myself concerned about Daddy. I hadn't seen him cry and he was quieter than before. He would stand at the window for an hour in the dusk, as though looking, or listening, for the fall of chestnuts on the lawn; when I switched on the light he would turn to me with a look of indescribably melancholy longing. I told Finny it would be another while yet. "Fine," he said.

He had a gig in Dublin at Hallowe'en; I went along, but found the atmosphere raw and unsettling, and afterwards, in his B&B,

I wasn't able for the wilder shores; I just cried like a child in his arms. I knew I would feel safe with him back in Cork, but I dreaded telling Daddy. For a fortnight I sought the courage, and then I blurted it out. Daddy looked at me in silence for seconds, then said, "You can't be serious."

The silence was repeated, then he left the room.

I began to strain at the leash. My concern for Daddy's welfare was waning, but I wasn't able just to walk out. I said that to Finny when I phoned him.

"Take your time, girl, take all the time you need," he said; that made me keener than ever. The next day I told Daddy I'd be leaving shortly.

"That's dangerous talk," he said.

"What do you mean?" I asked him.

"I don't have to spell it out for you," he answered.

I wished he would spell it out, yet I was afraid to know what he meant. And I didn't leave. There were no locks to hold me, but I was a prisoner. I played Finny's music and lost weight.

Daddy wanted us to be away for Christmas, so we went to a hotel in Rosslare. I barely touched turkey or pudding, I spent all my time alone. On Stephen's Day I walked by the sea for hours, mixing my tears with the spray. The following day I walked again, read, and retired early. I sat in bed in the dark, listening to some of Finny's slow airs. Around midnight I was fiddling with the tape-recorder when there was a knock on my door. I put the recorder on the floor and said, "Come in." My father entered, wearing a dressing-gown, and sat on the bed; I could smell brandy.

"You still want to go back to your piper?" he asked.

"Yes," I said.

"Well, you can, on one condition."

"What's that?"

"That you let me make love to you."

I let him.

I took the first train to Dublin, packed my things, and drove in Mummy's car to Cork. There was a new lock on Finny's door. When he opened to me, he looked alarmed, but I put my head on his chest anyway and sobbed. After a while he held me at arm's length and said, "Things have changed, Cora." I hardly heard, and I told him what I'd done to come back to him.

He stood back, horrified, and said, "Jesus, Cora, you didn't expect me to come into you after that, did you? Jesus, Cora, that's fucking disgusting. Fuck me!"

I couldn't answer, I couldn't speak. Then he told me he had met someone else. In September. I collapsed on the stairs, choking. He left me there; I heard him walk away. He returned shortly after with two big black plastic bags: my clothes and other belongings. He actually left them out on the pavement. Somehow I found myself beside them. I'm not even sure he said goodbye.

I drove, I don't know how, I didn't know where. After a couple of hours, a sign for Adare rang a bell: a college friend, Fiona, lived there; I found her. She gave me a stiff brandy and put me to bed; all I could say was that my boyfriend had dumped me.

I stayed a week with Fiona, nursing my grief and my shame. I told her little, except that I wanted to live quiet and alone. An aunt of hers, she said, owned a cottage in North Clare, near Bell Harbour, and needed a caretaker; I volunteered for the job. I would look after the place and have free lodgings, and I could live by signing on. I arranged that any urgent communication from my father could come through Fiona; he must not be told my whereabouts. To make myself less traceable, I went to a dealer in Limerick and exchanged Mummy's car for another. I began my new life on the feast of Women's Christmas.

Care of the cottage was simple, but I attended to it with puritan rigour, tolerating neither dirt nor dust. I read. I tramped the stony hills for three or four hours a day. My obsession was the half-acre behind the house: I wanted it stripped down to the rock. Every flower and weed and tiny thorny tree I ripped out by the roots, and as spring advanced I was merciless to each new shoot. When summer was coming in, I had the baldest backyard in the Burren.

I didn't wash. Myself I mean. I wanted proof that I was as dirty as I felt. In the dole queue one day the word "crusty" was muttered behind me. I didn't mind, actually I got a kick out of it.

One day I walked over Abbey Hill and came down to Corcomroe. It was my first visit, though it's only a few miles from the cottage; I tend to avoid churchy places. I liked the peace there, and I learned from a plaque that the Abbey was known as Sancta Maria de Petra Fertile, St Mary's of the Fertile Rock. I thought it a lovely name, and on my way home I found myself singing over and over, in a kind of Gregorian chant: "Sancta Maria de Petra Fertile, ora pro nobis." It became my mantra in the weeks that followed, and I chanted it especially while policing my patch, defending my precious grey against upstart green.

Via Fiona, I received a letter from my father. He was engaged to be married to a jeweller from Newbridge named Alison Nugent; he hoped we could be reconciled, and that the enclosed cheque might help in this regard. The cheque was for £5000. I was about to tear it up when something told me it could be a weapon.

Four hours later I was facing a 30 year-old Alison Nugent across her counter; she was attaching a clasp to a string of pearls. I told her the kind of man she was engaged to, and what he had done in Rosslare. She didn't believe me, of course, until I placed my tape-recorder on the counter and pressed 'play'. She recognised his voice, and listened, shocked, to the whole episode, from the heavy breathing, the creaking, the grunting, to the whimpering, the footsteps leaving, and the sobbing going on and on . . . She wept. After a long time she said, "You poor child, you poor child."

There would be no wedding, and she was most grateful. She

wanted to give me something. I declined but she pressed a large pearl into my palm. She would have embraced me, I'm sure, but for my smell.

On my way home I tried to pick the best place for the pearl: a window-sill in the sun, a bowl on a low table, a hole or a crack in a rock . . . I fell into bed in the small hours, undecided.

When I awoke in the morning, I moved like one emerging from hypnosis; I sought out the swimsuit Jean-Christophe had given me, and glued Alison Nugent's pearl into the crotch. I appended a note saying: '*Pearl of great price*', wrapped and addressed the lot and brought it to the Post Office. Then I phoned a recording studio in Galway and booked their editing facilities for the next day. (An offer to pay more than the going rate jumped me to the head of the queue.) I then listened all day to my recordings of Finny's music, and with an eye to beauty and variety of melody, brilliance of playing, acceptable recording quality, and absence of copyright problems, I made an album-length selection of tunes.

The next few weeks brought an exhilaration I hadn't known since Brittany. After the editing came arrangements for the pressing of CDs and the copying of tapes, the writing of sleeve notes and delicate dealings with printers. At every stage the chequebook worked miracles.

On a Friday night I drove home knackered and ecstatic with a thousand CDs and a thousand cassettes, all packaged, in the car. It was dark when I arrived and a strong wind was blowing from the sea. I delayed before entering the house; in my exalted mood I faced the wind and bellowed Shelley's ode: *O wild West Wind, thou breath of Autumn's being* . . . But I couldn't get beyond the first verse, and stood there repeating the last line of it, like Joxer with "*She is far from the land*": *Destroyer and Preserver; Hear, o hear!*

I was still chanting that when I had my first visitor in seven months. It was Jean-Christophe.

To my first question he answered: "The postmark was legible. Your embassy pinpointed the place on a map."

To my second question his answer was: "I sensed your distress. I recognised my role in it."

His English was fluent.

I told him my story, starting with Finny in The Thatch. I cried a lot about my mother and about Rosslare, but when I got to Finny and the plastic bags I lost control; I went and lay on my bed and sobbed. After a while Jean-Christophe followed me and put an arm around me. I pushed him away and said, "Can't you see I'm filthy? I stink."

I fell asleep soon after. When I awoke, towards dawn, I was *in* the bed and so was Jean-Christophe, and we were both in our underwear, and he had his arms around me, and he was snoring like a seal. I lay there in wonder and let myself be soothed, restored, as though by the balm of Bach or Mozart. At length I disengaged myself and went to take a shower; I returned to bed naked and wrapped myself around him again. I listened to the birds until he woke.

"Are you going to confess this?" I asked him.

He grinned.

"Are you still going to be a priest?"

He smiled. "I hope so." And then he added, "But who knows?"

When we rose, I was surprised by the amount of green that had grown among the stones behind the house.

"Your work can wait," he said at breakfast. "Over the next twelve days we are going to drive around the coast of Ireland, anticlockwise; each day we are going to swim on a beautiful beach, from which we will each bring home a beautiful white stone."

And we did that; in Kilkee, Glenbeigh, Glandore, Tramore, Arklow, Laytown, Donaghadee, Portrush, Magheraroarty, Rosses Point, Carrownisky, Dog's Bay. It was a beautiful time, with all the laughter I'd known in Paris, and all the kindness, plus the comfort of his arms round me at night.

Before I drove him to Shannon Airport, we went out in the early morning behind the house. There was growth everywhere. I carried my white stones in my dress: I scattered some like seeds, planted more like flowers, hid a couple. Jean-Christophe did the round of the boundary wall, stooping, rooting, planting.

"A necklace of a dozen white stones," I said when he'd finished.

"Thirteen," he answered. "your pearl is there somewhere too."

At the airport one last laugh was at a slip of his tongue: "In three weeks I'll be back in the cemetery." As he walked away from me, all waves and smiles, he looked like a boy scout going on jamboree.

I travelled the country again, hitting every city and decent-sized town. By the end of August I'd placed Finny's album in two hundred shops. I never gave my own name; I was simply Pearl, Pearl White, if I was pressed. When my stocks were almost exhausted, I posted two dozen CDs to my father from Cork GPO. Witch Doctor Productions 001 should interest him – the producer, according to the cover, being Dr Richard Stone, Stillorgan. I included a note saying: "*If you can't get rid of these, you could try them for sexual relief*". All the way home I played and replayed Finny's tape. Over and over I savoured the most deliciously excruciating experience I knew. The fruits of my hours in the editing studio: the unbearable squeals of long-drawn-out false notes; the infuriating changes in tempo; the inexplicable gaps in tunes; the murderous key-changes; the inclusion of one awful *untouched* track, recorded when Finny was pissed . . . And snaking in and out through it all, barging crudely in between tunes, writhing grotesquely on top of them, my father's heavy breathing, his grunting, his gasping, his groaning . . . In all this I took exquisite pleasure, as if watching him felled by a kidney stone.

Back in my own bed, my sleep was fitful. I got up at first light and drove down to the Flaggy Shore. I stripped and dressed in Finny's tape: i.e. I took a dozen cassettes from their boxes, ripped out the ribbons of tape and wrapped them round me; two round each leg, two round my hips, four round my trunk, and one round each arm. I dressed my head and face in a thirteenth tape – the one I'd made in Rosslare; then I walked blind into the sea and swam towards the lights of Galway. I went out a quarter of a mile, trailing ribbons of glory as I went. Then I thrashed and turned and plunged and wriggled and rolled till I was free; the face-mask was the last thing to come off. I sported and played for a long time, enjoying the freedom of myself and singing: "*Phoque, petit phoque, petit phoque, petit phoque.*" When I turned for shore the sun was up, and the first thing I saw was my house, nestling in a pale patch of green. "I'll make you flower!" I shouted. "I'll make you flower; you'll have orchids and gentians and loosestrife and fuchsia and montbretia and bloody cranesbill and bloody everything!"

Before I moved off I completed my offering to the sea: I threw in the empty cassettes with their inlay cards and plastic cases. Finny's photograph bobbed pathetically up and down – it's the one in which he most looks like Charles Manson – and three sweet words danced lightly and laughed up at me thirteen times: "The Mermaid's Revenge."

That was last Sunday.

Allow me to append a few comments, Prince. Considering these stories as so many waking dreams, I tend very simply to trace their origins to some prosaic elements of my own existence. In the present instance, the following facts account for much of the fiction: my father, a pathologist, had spent some time in a seminary and played the uileann pipes badly; I heard an archive recording of his 'Gold Ring' on radio last Saturday. I still possess the pearl necklace he gave my mother when they married; the large centre pearl was added to celebrate my birth. At a deeper level, I detect in Cora's mobility and her eventual sinking of roots a mild parallel to my own experience. In my childhood the family moved house three times; I attended two boarding-schools and two universities, and held six teaching posts before settling in the job I have occupied for the past fifteen years. I have never felt a strong or sentimental attachment to any place; it is my detachment, which explains that clinical precision for which I am noted in my work as placenames officer with the local County Council. (No other commentator has evinced that clarity of vision, which enables me to contemplate the corpus of anglicized Gaelic placenames as a mixture of poetry, pathos and farce.)

But I digress. I have kept you too long from the dust and sun of Sicily and the arms and charms of Venus.

I am

Yours respectfully,

Enda Ring.

LOVER

Dear Kate,

I remember your arrival at the Big House; I had arrived a day earlier as tutor to Miss Iris. The story was that you had been deposed as head of your order in Peru for failing to implement instructions from your superiors, then expelled after harrowing interrogation in Rome; you looked a fright. Your family were distant connections of the Morgan-Campbells, and had sent you to their place to recuperate.

I remember you, in the first few weeks, pottering around, feeding the cats, dusting. Then two things happened simultaneously, only one of which you were aware of: you conceived a passion for the gardener, and I developed an obsession for Miss Iris; we were each twice the age of our beloveds. I was keenly aware of my situation's potential for scandal; you seemed oblivious to the risk of ridicule. A fine-looking woman of 45, your colour returning, you bubbled like a teenager, skipping round the flowerbeds after Frankie. Do you remember? 'Frankie is pruning the roses today,' you'd proclaim, as though announcing the Second Coming, or 'If anyone is looking for me, I'll be composting the marrows with Frankie.' Meanwhile, I considered seeking release from my delicious *torture, but I needed the money. So I continued to tell Iris about Shelley and the trade winds and French verbs, plagued unrelentingly by notions of pushing books aside and devouring her lips and cheeks and neck and budding breasts . . . She never noticed: so she told me years later.*

I don't know whether you annoyed Frankie, but as the word got round, he became embarrassed, and made fun of you in the pub. 'You know what she did today, boys? She caught me in a half-nelson and shoved her diddy in my mouth.' Or 'Guess what, boys; didn't she whip off her knickers in the greenhouse and show me her arse!'

I was sitting down to my final class with Iris, just before the summer holidays, when a taxi pulled up outside the main door and you climbed in with a bulky suitcase and a pale tearstained face. You had gone home to your family, we were told; it was whispered that you were pregnant. Frankie left the job and the area, enlightening no-one.

Various rumours reached us: your family had put you – in the 70's! – in some kind of home; you'd had a miscarriage, a stillbirth, a Down's Syndrome baby girl . . . You'd had a breakdown and were in an asylum . . . I'd rather in fact not know what happened to you after you departed the Big House, or whether you have departed this life. The attached story might tell you something about me. Before you read it, though, let me acknowledge that you made a difference: had you not been in the Big House that year, I might well have done a very foolish thing.

Most of the women I've slept with would call me a male chauvinist pig; and they'd be right. But they'd agree as well that I'm a hell of a charmer. It was the unexpected discovery I made after leaving school, and I clocked up conquests with the delight of a paraplegic doing somersaults. By the age of 28 I'd had six fairly lengthy relationships, as well as dozens of briefer encounters, and what gave me particular pleasure was that nearly all of my partings had been amicable. I saw my second amorous decade following the same pattern; commitment could come with middle age. But I didn't foresee the challenge of total beauty suddenly appearing. Physical beauty, elegance, charm . . . yes, of course, but, allied to these, genuine goodness, virtuousness, *and* virginity; I took it all in a flash.

It happened in an art gallery in Galway, at the opening of an exhibition of Russian icons. Two women entered as the speeches were about to begin, and took up position a few feet ahead of me. One was a middle-aged matron, the other was twenty, and beauty incarnate! I saw no more icons that evening. That creamy region behind and below the ear, with its one wispy golden trespasser, that's what my eyes were locked on as the voices droned. I willed her to turn her head, and just once she did, to leave an empty wineglass on a sill. "Five minutes," I thought, "five minutes in your bed; for that I'd trade the thousand nights I've spent in others".

When informality resumed, I followed her every movement. I registered *everything*: the grave concentration she mustered to focus on an exhibit, the tilt of her chin as she turned, the shy vivaciousness in her eyes, the modest luminosity of her smile, the – this sounds ridiculous, I know – the *defencelessness* of her most un-Roman, supremely appealing nose . . . Description is pointless: the dimensions of the bulb can give no idea of the light. I wanted her.

I caught her eye; there was something quizzical in her look, something almost hinting at recognition. I approached her a little later, a glass of red wine in each hand. She shook her head, not smiling; her eyes said: "you silly man . . . but I'm used to silly men," or so I thought. For the first time in my career I was flummoxed. I turned away, discommoded by my two glasses. I contemplated drinking them both; instead I drank neither, and left.

I made enquiries, but no-one I knew knew her. I lost interest in other women, I thought about her all the time, her golden hair was what I most sought as I travelled up and down the country. (I dealt in antiques.) After five months I found her, managing a new antique shop in Limerick. I was embarrassed, she wasn't; she was reserved, correct and unsmiling. We talked shop, and I bought a sword and a little Chinese marble horseman. Her name was Regina Canny.

I called a fortnight later and took away two carved Malawi masks. On my third visit it was a Victorian chamberpot: that provoked a grin, a little split-second rainbow. I began concentrating my work in the southwest, and dropped in more or less weekly. She unstiffened; there was the odd smile, the occasional glimpse of a life, but when I asked her out I received a polite refusal. When I returned to the charge I learned that she was engaged. I couldn't bring myself to ask who to.

A few months later, the wedding photograph in *The Limerick Leader* informed me: Eusebius Tuffy, a well-known millionaire confectioner, corpulent, balding, pastyfaced, ineffectual-looking, 48 or 50. I freaked. I imagined myself setting fire to her – his – shop. I had five one-night stands in a fortnight. I drank, I drove like a maniac, declaiming obscene rhymes based on her name. I vilified Mr Sweetballs too, though the rhymes were less satisfactory; but oh how much I envied him, Jesus how I envied that tub of lard. One day near Crusheen I lost a wing mirror to a truck; that sobered me. I pulled in and cried till my sweater was sopping.

I avoided Limerick. Eventually I calmed. But I couldn't settle; I was obsessed. Picking up women in nightclubs, I imagined each time it was Regina, and the killer always was that it wasn't; I'd have been better off playing chess. I floundered for months in self-pity. Then a former girlfriend advised me to wise up. I tried instead to toughen up; I told myself that all might not be lost, that Regina might soon have a bellyful of her sugarhubby. I began calling on her again.

I proceeded gently: I always did business; not till about the sixth visit did I risk admiring her earrings. Gradually she unbent; we chatted more easily, there was the occasional laugh. One day she joined me for a coffee and enjoyed herself. I launched more compliments after that, and more personal ones; she was embarrassed, but pleased. A few times I enquired about Mr Tuffy; there were references to his work, nothing personal, nothing that brought a light to her eye. At lunch on my birthday I decided to go for it: I proposed a night together, some time when Eusebius would be away. She knocked over her wineglass and, some seconds later, expressed outrage. A week later I asked again, stressing how much I loved her; she became quite agitated, and blushed to her necklace. The next time I called, another woman was managing the shop; Regina would not be back. I phoned her some time later at her home; she did not wish to meet me. I engineered a chance meeting in the street, and she jumped in a taxi. I sent her a gift – an etching of a horsewoman riding into the sea; she returned it.

I took a flat in Limerick. For a month I did nothing but make her see me. I made her see me in her church on Sunday by attending every Mass. I made her see me in the Belltable Theatre by being present at every performance. I made her see me at a book-launch, I made her see me at a concert, I made her see me in the post office, in the supermarket, at a service station. I watched her grow more and more embarrassed. I crashed a party I knew she'd be at and handed her a note: "*I love you more than ever and I want a lot more than one night.*" She left the room and I lost sight of her for weeks.

My patience grew thin. One night – it was in September '88 – I entered her back garden and made my way to the rear of the house. A window was open and she and Tuffy were talking. She was pleading with him to take her to live in England. He talked about business. I missed bits – he had his back to me – then he was saying something about her mother. Her reply was clear: "I know she's your best friend as well as mine, but our marriage is more important than her feelings, and our marriage is at risk if we stay here." His response was muffled, then – you wouldn't believe this if you read it in a novel – she said, with real anguish, that she was in danger of losing her heart to another man. There was a silence, then a question, and I caught the words "pursuing me . . . won't leave me alone." He asked, with the voice of a man on his death bed, "Who . . . ?" And the answer came in bits, like a broken tooth: "A . . . a customer in the shop . . . , an antique dealer . . . , a Mr Moore from Clara." And then the sweetest sounds of the night: her sobbing, his silence.

For a while I kept a low profile. I was still pondering my next move when at Hallowe'en, Eusebius Tuffy, millionaire confectioner, died suddenly. I ensured that she saw me at the funeral, but I kept my distance. Shortly afterwards I wrote a note of condolence: I would always be there, if she needed me.

In the New Year I risked a respectable phone call; she said, "You killed my husband," and put down the receiver.

A month later she was back in the shop, and she apologised for that outburst, but she held herself aloof. Gradually, though, as twice before, she thawed, although to a lesser extent. Eventually I told her I loved her, and she brushed my declaration aside. I renewed my attack once or twice, until one day she sat me down, stood over me and, with the utmost seriousness, said, "Oisín, you're wasting your time. I don't deny that I have feelings for you, and, in other circumstances, who knows what might have happened? But things are as they are. And there's something else: I don't trust you. You say you love me; I don't doubt that you're sincere, and I appreciate the compliment. But if I gave in to you, you'd lose interest. What drives you is the thrill of the chase; after the kill you'd be sniffing round for another quarry. What keeps you keen is the fact that I won't yield."

I left her alone for some months and gave up my Limerick flat, but one wet autumn afternoon I decided to call again to the shop. It wasn't there; I found a bevy of helmeted ladies in a hairdresser's. I drove straight to her house. An elderly maid told me she was in a convent. On a visit? I asked. On a retreat? No, she was a nun now, she was after entering a strict order above in Cavan: "Oh, she looked like a princess and she leaving us, and we won't see her again this side of heaven." And the old woman produced a pair of tears.

They were nothing to what I produced in the days that followed. I tried to revive my obscene rhymes, but they fell flat. I moped, I lay in bed; mostly I lay in bed. Once I roused myself in the night and hunted for that convent in Cavan; I attended Mass there at dawn, imagining Regina a few feet and a wall away. Embarrassment at that episode was what ejected me eventually from my stupor. I got back on the road.

By the following Christmas I was in a relationship with a woman named Niamh; in June I married her. (She was four months pregnant.) We settled in Portumna. I took to marriage like a swan to a duck-pond. Our son Finbar was born that November. Business kept me busy. Life was what I expected: no great shakes.

Less than twelve months later came a shake that was very great: I ran into Regina. In a hotel in Connemara; she was recovering from her mother's death, and readjusting after leaving the convent. Her superiors had been sceptical about her vocation from the start; after six months they counselled her to leave, but allowed her to stay as a lay helper; when a year was up they insisted she return to the world. I spoke gently, and said little.

I was gentle the next time we met too, and the next time, and the time after that. (She was back in Limerick by then.) I reined in hand and eye, I was all ear and gravely nodding head. She was grateful, easing back into life. Out of nowhere, it seemed, a cry came one evening as I rose to leave: "Oh, Oisín, I could never marry you, you know that!"

"We don't need to be married," I said quietly, "in order to share our love."

"That's even less possible," she said, "I can't live with you and with God."

"We must stop seeing each other, then?"

"I'm afraid so", she said, "but not yet, oh please, not yet."

I delayed my next visit for a fortnight; we became lovers. She was a virgin. Many a night in the convent, she told me, she had wept in her cell, trying to banish images of me.

It was like first love all over again. And the spectacle of her passion battling with embarrassment and scruples gave my desire an edge it hadn't had for years. I contrived to be with her twice, three times a week. Yet I was away from Niamh no more frequently than before. I felt little or no guilt; my family, I was certain, was benefiting from my high spirits. Niamh became pregnant again.

The summer was glorious. I took days off work, spent days and nights with Regina all over the south and west. Aspects of her I hadn't been aware of showed themselves: her good humour, and her sudden displays of high spirits; once, in a hotel foyer, as we waited for our bedroom keys, she did a sudden impromptu tap-dance on the parquet, bringing a smile to the receptionist's face and a blush to mine. It was gratifying to see her acquiring the habit of pleasure. Once she paused during our lovemaking and asked, "You won't grow tired of me, Oisín, will you?"; without waiting for an answer, she bit me, hard, on the stomach. Half an hour later, I had scarcely the energy to tell her she had tired me already. And that she was more beautiful than I'd ever seen her before.

One night in August I arrived in Portumna to find the house empty. On the kitchen table was a suitcase with some of my clothes, and a note saying: "*Take your sweet teeth back to Sister Toffee-tits, they'll nibble my neck no more.*"

I drove to Niamh's mother's place and was told by two screaming women never to show my face again.

Illogically, I told Regina. She was horrified to learn that I was married.

"It doesn't matter," I told her. "It wasn't relevant, that's why I didn't tell you; you didn't want to marry me anyway."

"But we're wronging your wife!" she said; "I didn't know that till now; you must give me up."

"She won't take me back," I said.

"I'll talk to her."

And she did. And got nowhere. But she broke with me anyway. For a month. Then she phoned me:

"I'm weak; as long as Niamh won't have you, I want you."

I proposed moving in with her, but she wanted more discretion. By November we were settled in the Lake District, near Ambleside. Regina opened an antique shop; I travelled; we rented a cottage with a garden.

It was strange, the quiet, the end of chasing and dodging; we were even a bit shy of each other. Then it dawned on us: our happiness was our own house; there was nobody threatening eviction. Everything we shared became quiet delight: shopping, cooking, reading, lakeshore walks . . . Our lovemaking was relaxed and still magical. We laughed, at times to paroxysm, on provocations undeniably slight. Like when she told me to scrub the area between the head and the shoulders generally known as the neck . . . Or when a newspaper headline proclaimed: "*Wife Knifes Farting Husband. Bedroom Was Gas-Chamber, Says Defiant Granny.*" Or most spectacularly and unaccountably of all, when the wrapper on a cake instructed us to "*Keep this delicacy in a bread-bin.*"

Christmas was a sensitive time. And Niamh gave birth to Grainne a few weeks later; her anger with me reached new heights and my brother warned me not to attend the christening. Regina insisted I go home around Patrick's Day and ask to be taken back. I was appalled.

"For my sake," she said. "For the love of me."

I couldn't fathom that. I hoped Niamh would bawl me out, and she did. She wouldn't even let me see the children. My brother told me to stay away and keep paying the bills; Niamh had a violent streak.

I had fewer qualms now. I threw myself into our shared life and love as if I'd been put on earth for nothing else. And we had a perfect year: we tasted the tang of every shift of the seasons, from the daffodils through the sensual summer, to the nudity of winter and back to the crocuses: I have never known a year so like a life. And I was happy. Yet, as I drained glass after exquisite glass, I occasionally found a bitter drop in the bottom.

In April of last year Regina became ill. Leukaemia was diagnosed, acute. She had chemotherapy – a week each month for three months. The first time, once she got over her nausea, she arranged for her solicitor to come from Limerick, to sort out her affairs. I protested, she insisted, it was done. Returning to hospital, she asked me to go and see Niamh again. I refused, said she was crazy.

"I won't be asking you many more favours", she said. "Tell Niamh I want her to take you back when I'm gone."

I went, and managed to deliver the message; Niamh listened, and shut the door without a reply.

Regina's third bout of chemo was in June. Discharging her, the doctors said they would do a bone marrow transplant in mid-July. She smiled at that.

She was listless for a week or so, but on Sunday the nineteenth she perked up; she was in better form than I'd seen her for months, and she managed a little walk.

That evening, after I'd settled her in her bed, she asked me to bring her some fuchsia from the hedge.

"*Deora Dé*," she said when I put a branch in her hand. "*Deora Dé*, that's what they're called in Irish, God's tears."

"And *Lacrima Christi*, Christ's tears, is the name of two Italian wines," I said. *Rosso* and *bianco*. Can't you see Christ letting the white flow when the red runs out? No more *Sangre de Toro*, the bull is dead and bled. Am I blaspheming?"

"And a ladybird in Irish is *bó Dé*, God's cow", she went on.

"Odd," I quipped, "that God's cows are smaller than his tears."

"I'm not surprised," she answered, "I'm not surprised at all."

There was a silence.

"You know, Oisín," she said after a while, "I'd have broken off my engagement with Eusebius and gone with you, but for one thing . . . one person."

"Who?"

"Heather Kelly."

I froze. Heather Kelly was a girlfriend I'd got pregnant in 1984: she wanted me to marry her: I offered her the price of an abortion, and she hanged herself.

"She was a foolish girl," I muttered.

"She was my first cousin," Regina said, "and a good friend. You'd have met me three years earlier if you'd been at her funeral."

The silence this time was a long one. Eventually she squeezed my hand, smiling.

"I've had a good life," she said. "I've had the love of two good men and learned – or heard, anyway – a little about the love of God."

"Very different things, I suppose?" I said.

"Utterly," was her answer; "like shadow and sun, but related, like shadow to sun."

Then she told me to bring a bottle of white wine from the fridge, and two glasses.

"But you can't drink," I said.

"Two glasses," she repeated.

I obeyed, and filled the glasses. I offered her one.

"You drink for both of us," she said.

I sipped from the two glasses alternately and dropped tears in them, and we looked at each other in silence. It was a good half-hour.

"Would you like," she asked me then, "to put your delicacy in my bread-bin, one last time? . . . I mean it. You're welcome to."

She might as well have asked me to knife her. For the first time in my life I declined that particular invitation. I did so laughing and crying, and she joined me, and our embrace was our most perfect ever act of love.

"Could you bring me the icon from the kitchen?", she asked me around 9.00.

When I got up to go she said, "Kiss me." I did. Intimately, tenderly. In the kitchen I took down the icon; it left the ghost of a pale rectangle on the wall. I looked at the face of Christ; I had never done so properly before. "Expressionless," I thought at first. "It says nothing." Then it struck me that, like the Buddha's smile, its nothing might be everything as well: the Irish word *folamh* came to mind. "Severe," I thought then, "but fair." "God is fair," I remembered my first girlfriend telling me, a German named Christina; she was trying to assuage the guilt I felt at my first taste of sex, balancing it against the savaging I'd suffered from flesh-hating clerical educators.

Returning to the bedroom I held the icon aloft and did a mock churchy chant: "*For my yoke is easy and my burden light.*" There was no answer. She had slipped away. It was less than seven years since I'd found her golden hair among the antiques. I lay beside her, took her in my arms and stroked her, murmuring her name, for the last time inhaling her fragrance, wetting her face and hair with my tears.

Later I noticed on the back of the icon, in Regina's handwriting: *The Word was made flesh, and dwelt amongst us,* and underneath that, *Jesus, lover of sinners.*

Niamh wrote last November: "*Oisín, come home.*"

I did. I was introduced to the children and given the spare room. I got used to a diet of dust and ashes, but Finbar and Grainne were moisture. Then in February Finbar got meningitis, and died in hospital. Niamh screamed that it was all my fault, then shot the paediatrician. She has been in custody for the past seven months, and undergoing psychiatric tests. I see her every weekend; she doesn't say much.

What went wrong? What is wrong, that makes things go wrong? Trying to trace causes is like pulling a thread and unravelling a suit. Original Sin strikes me as plausible, but it hardly strengthens the case that God is fair.

I hope I die soon.

He's a stalker, Kate, isn't he? I know something about something like that.

I had a couple of breakdowns, caused partly by my feelings for Miss Iris. But I got on with things, had flings. And then I bumped into her – a thirteen-year-old turned nineteen overnight. I told her how I'd felt about her in her gym-frock days, and we laughed. The words were scarcely out of my mouth when I burned with desire for her again. I tracked her down shortly afterwards in Trinity, and told her; she was gracious but in no mood for nonsense.

To keep myself distracted, I undertook a search for a college classmate for whose disappearance years earlier I blamed myself. Holidays had just begun. I drove every day to one or two towns; erratically, systematically, I combed the streets, checked every shop, pub, church and public place. And always as in a race against time: my tyres screeched as I set off for the next place: Athlone, Roscommon, Longford, Carrick-on-Shannon, Ballinasloe, Ennis, Westport . . .

One dripping July evening, exhausted, I entered a pub in Rooskey, ordered a pint, and sat in the darkest corner. An attractive blonde approached, slid in beside me, all smiles, and said: 'You're a man who's hopelessly in love, right?' 'Yes,' I said, taken aback. 'I'm Sarah,' she said, 'and I've got one mighty merit your beloved doesn't.' 'What's that?' I questioned, defensively. 'Availability,' she answered. 'And what do you do, Sarah?' I asked, the first question I could think of. 'I'm the poultry instructress,' she said, laughing, as she slipped her hand under my bum. Then we were both laughing, it was my first time in ages, and the search for my classmate was called off.

I moved in with Sarah that night, and we had the grandest dirty summer you could imagine, until we made a baby – or so she claimed, demanding my hand in marriage. I proposed abortion instead, and she turned into a tornado, volcano, tsunami and massive mudslide all in one. I scooted, glad she couldn't track me, as I was changing employment and abode. And within days my mind was full again of Iris.

I couldn't approach her directly, so I took to haunting the centre of Dublin every weekend. I met her once and we exchanged friendly words: pure happiness, with pain to follow. Months passed, and three things happened. I thought I saw my missing classmate, (and dived into a shop.) I saw Sarah, ten yards away, not obviously pregnant. I saw Iris once more, kissing another woman on O' Connell Bridge. I was in hospital within the week.

Life resumed. I changed jobs, moved in with my ageing parents. They died. I married. At 47, with six kids, am I cured of Miss Iris? I am not. At every moment I am dying to see her. Everywhere outside my own door I seek her. I consider her, not the woman I married, as my true, my real wife. I'm tempted to believe there's a heaven, on the basis that I'm destined eventually to enjoy her.

Sorry, Kate, I got carried away. What I've told you is irrelevant to Oisín's story, most of which looks like a lift from a few French novels.

Yours affectionately,

Enda Ring.

HERO

Dear Monsieur Camus,

Secular saint, conscience of France, man of integrity, truth-teller, prose stylist . . . all hail!

In college I read and loved your fiction, but didn't bother with your philosophy or journalism. I was influenced by a lecturer's comment: 'Of course, anyone who has that much affection and respect for his parents can't possibly be a serious thinker.' The statement saddened me on two counts: first, that you weren't a serious thinker, second, that you were fond of your parents. Defensively, my affection for you deepened. You became for me – mostly through hearsay – the just, the honest man, and so you remained for decades.

A few years ago I visited the lecturer in hospital; her ancient father was present. She bemoaned the dearth of philosophical comment on contemporary hedonism. 'That's right,' her father said, 'there's no brains goin' nowadays at all, only all balls an' boobs.' 'Someone like Camus is needed,' the lecturer cut in. But, I asked, hadn't she told us you weren't a serious thinker? Oh, she was, of course, she said, speaking tongue in cheek.

I didn't have the heart after that to tackle your non-fiction. As *an intellectual pygmy, I reasoned, I wouldn't be able for it anyway. What's more, I've grown sceptical of your personal integrity. In fact, I've fallen out with you. And, to tell the truth, I don't believe you're such a major thinker after all. And I'm angry that you're not. And that you're not a larger figure on the world stage. All right, you helped steer intellectual debate in France for two decades, but ultimately, what mark have you left? Whereas that other footballer – wasn't he a goalie too? – who also dabbled in theatre, he has encased the Rock of Peter in two thousand megatons of concrete, and has changed the course of history more surely than a mile-wide asteroid crashing into the planet. It's enough to make one weep.*

I've read your fictions; could you find the time to read one of mine?

As a child I knew that I was special: it was clear from my wonderful beginnings. The night after I was born – at home, 1 February 1950 – my mother rose in a delirium from her bed – my father was in the pub – and, imagining some danger, tried to carry me to a nearby holy well. On the bridge behind the house she fainted, and I ended up in the river. And that would have been that, only for Winnie Willie; she was crossing the stepping-stones a mile downstream when I floated, prim and placid, to her feet. She gathered me in her arms and baptized me in the river there and then. 'Joy' was the name she gave me: she'd seen two magpies at the spot some time before. The parish priest baptized me conditionally the following Sunday; he wouldn't trust Winnie Willie to do it right. But they left me my name: Joy.

School bored me. Church too. The sacraments I cared for were from elsewhere. Mist moving over the river in the mornings: I thought that was the meaning of 'mystery'. Birds singing: with them around, what hymns could God want, what God could want hymns? And my first snowdrops – my mother showed them to me, inside the cemetery wall, on black clay under bare beeches – it was to them I'd have liked to make my first confession.

The year of my First Communion, repairs were carried out on our house; part of a ceiling was demolished, and honey came pouring from the attic. My mother ran around with buckets and basins; workmen sucked honeycombs, with bees crawling on their fingers, near their lips; my father drank bottles of stout and laughed looking on. For a while, I thought heaven was in the attic.

I was ten when I found the stone. I was helping my father at a potato pit when it fell from a lump of clay into my hand. Red sandstone, the size of a hazelnut, and roughly hemispherical. And embedded in the curved surface, perfectly centred, the imprint of a tiny scallop shell. We lived 50 miles from the sea. My father grunted. My mother told me the stone had been left there 10,000 years ago by melting ice, but it was millions of years since it was formed from the sand the shell had lain in; my hand was the first hand ever to hold it. She told me too that the scallop shell was a symbol of the pilgrim, and she talked about St James of Compostela; before I could ask her she said Compostela was the field of the star. I made a pouch for the stone, with a leather thong for hanging round my neck; I resolved to wear it forever and ever and ever. With my scapulars and miraculous medal, though, my chest was a bit crowded, so I laid aside my scapulars and I bore my new gift like a star.

When I was in Confirmation class, a white blackbird appeared around the school. For most of the pupils it was a one-day wonder, but I stayed on after school every day, hoping for a glimpse of the miracle. One evening I was crouched in the playground with a stomach cramp, contemplating the apparition, when a commotion put it to flight, and James Costello appeared, catapult swinging. James's father employed my father, and owned our cottage. James was older than me, and bigger, but I had flattened him before he saw me. He recovered, and pinned me to the ground. My dress came up and he began to pull down my knickers: incongruously, my hands went to my chest. Suddenly he backed away in disgust, and I saw my first woman's blood. He ran, and I went to wash in the river.

During my teenage years my main teacher was Winnie Willie. My father warned me occasionally to stay away from 'that whore', but as his drinking grew worse, he paid me little attention. It was her horses that drew me to Winnie first; she had two, and she rode with a passion that I longed to attain myself. But there was a total absorption in *everything* she did, her gardening, her cookery, her DIY . . . While offering me her knowledge, she seemed somehow oblivious to my presence. And never more so than when she sang. It would be unannounced and uncommented on; it could be in Irish or in English; it often came on her as she stood at a door or a window, as though fixing some point of memory in the landscape. I would listen spellbound, with not the slightest idea that this could in any way be imitable. All I could have said was that it symbolized the life she led: full, intense, self-sufficient, and confined. She had no friends except myself; because she had been a prostitute in the time of the copper-mine, she was the pariah of the parish of Dysart.

I left school after my Inter Cert. because I'd had enough of James Costello's eyes. We never spoke or exchanged looks, but whenever he was near me I felt naked.

I looked at my mother's purple eye one morning and asked her why she'd married my father.

"Your father gave me a life," she said. "He took me out of the Good Shepherd Convent when I was three months pregnant by another man." My real father was a priest; she would reveal no more. I said I would no longer be Molloy; I would take her name, Greene. She laughed.

"Why not Derrig after my mother, or Canty after granny Canty, or Cassidy after *her* mother, Bridget Cassidy?"

She could go no further back, and for a while I did call myself Joy Cassidy.

Winnie brought me to the Ballinasloe Horse Fair that autumn, and I went to a fortune-teller, Madam Joan.

"Bridget Cassidy's mother's name was Lucy Kehoe," she said as soon as I sat down.

"And *her* mother was Agnes Wilson, and *her* mother was Isobel Gargan, and *her* mother was Julia Sweeney, and *her* mother was Grace Hennessy, and *her* mother was Mary Deasy. And *her* mother," – here there was a pause and a smile – "was Joan Molloy. And that takes you back to the time of the Wild Geese."

I produced my pound note without a word, and she held it in the flame of a candle. She rubbed the ashes into my hair and said, "Go and wash in your own river and you'll find your own name."

That night I bathed near the stepping-stones, while Winnie held a torch. I came out shivering and I tried to say: "I'm perishing", but the words Winnie heard were: "I'm Pickering." So for the second time she christened me: I'm Pickering.

A little thing happened next morning; not important, but I remember. I was standing naked in front of my wardrobe mirror. The sun was shining, and for ages I took pleasure in my hair and eyes and face. I rotated to view my breasts at different angles. I admired my hips and thighs, and my little dusky bush that seemed to want to shine and yet be shy. I had done all these things before, but not the next thing: I stepped over to the mirror and kissed myself.

Two things happened on my seventeenth birthday: my father had a stroke, which put him in a wheel-chair, and my mother got word of a legacy: a cousin in the States had put an end to any money worries we could ever have.

The following Easter Sunday there was drama when Father MacManamon was giving out Communion. An emaciated greyhound entered the chapel with a tin can tied to his tail and proceeded to hobble up the aisle; a more pathetic sight I had never seen. Nobody moved till he reached the altar rails. Father Mac got a start and dropped a host. The dog snapped it up. Then James Costello leaped from the front seat and kicked the poor devil hard, twice; he yelped and came limping back. I left my place, took him in my arms and walked out. I borrowed my parents' Morris Minor and headed for Winnie's.

"Holy Moses!" was her first comment on the dog, and Moses became his name. We freed him and fed him and gave him a bed near the fire. Every evening till he was well I stroked him to sleep. He lapped up life like milk.

Walking home one evening I saw a star fall. It crackled: a good omen. But what I heard was our house burning: around the next corner I saw the flames.

I found them unconscious on their bedroom floor. I hoisted my father on my back and carried him out the front door. I was unable to go in a second time. He died too before help came, a bottle-opener clutched in his good hand. They were buried on 1 May.

Forensic tests on the house proved inconclusive. Moses went missing the night of the fire and was never seen again.

I moved in with Winnie. She was my rock, my fortress, the oak I leaned against, giving birth to myself. For the first time she told me her story, giving a new slant to gossip. She lost her mother at ten, her negligent spendthrift father at eighteen; she was left with a house and a mere three fields, and a burning, all-consuming thirst for love. By twenty she had a live-in lover, was pregnant and happy. The lover was knifed by another miner, in a fight over another woman. She miscarried; as soon as she recovered, she slept with ten more men in a month. She was beaten up then, by my father's boss . . . and by my father; she spent time in a psychiatric hospital. For the past 25 years she had tried to live as though no other person existed . . . except me, of course; I was her daughter. My view of her turned inside out like a glove: she was as much a prisoner as my mother. And my pity helped crystallize my ambition: I would be above all a free woman, and I would fight above all to free women.

On my eighteenth birthday I set off in the Morris Minor, although there was snow on the ground. I took a road I hadn't travelled since the funerals. Outside our house there were piles of tiles and timber, and two workmen pottering around. In the cemetery I hunted for snowdrops and placed a bunch on my mother's grave.

A snow fight was in progress outside Costellos', but it was a stone that James let fly at me; it made a star of my right wing mirror and sent snow fanning over my windscreen, like champagne launching a ship.

For a year I was like a bird freed from a cage. I went everywhere, staying nowhere for more than days. In Glendalough I recognized my ideal place of rest, and decided to avoid it forever.

Then my mission began, in Galway, where I organized a strike among shop assistants for better conditions. There were self-defence classes for women, literacy lessons for travellers, a fight for crèche facilities in factories. I founded a babysitting agency. I picketed workplaces where women were sexually harassed. I persuaded some women to leave abusive partners . . .

I had an assistant for three years in all of this – a woman named Isobel Freeley. She was a bit too addicted to God for my liking, but she was a tireless worker. It was a blow when she entered some new kind of convent in Abbeyphelim. For several months I failed to replace her, then I visited the convent and asked her to return to useful work in the world. She spoke of the need for reparation for sin: she spent hours every day before the Blessed Sacrament. Did she not have doubts? Oh yes, she no longer understood why God should take offence at our misdeeds, but she supposed it was a compliment that He did, and she ploughed on praying in the dark. I couldn't make head or tail of that, and I couldn't see how it fitted with the puzzling motto chiselled over the convent entrance: DILIGE ET QUOD VIS FAC, which meant, I was told, Love and do what you wish.

And then I met Robin. Robin Avis: an English-born artist, 30ish, thin, dark, balding, intense, with wonderful brown eyes like bog pools. Within seconds I said to myself: "I'm spending my life with this man."

I decided to give him everything. I abandoned my campaigns: all causes would be served by loving Robin. I moved into his cottage near Enniscrone. That summer of '73 was idyllic.

I understood nothing of his art. He could stare at a landscape or the sea for hours, then pick up a brush and do nothing with it for as long again. Three or four tentative touches could be a day's work. Some canvasses he'd laid aside, you had to look hard to see paint on them at all; when I asked if they were finished, he wasn't sure. He'd go into great silences, and come back with a question like: "All art aspires to the condition of music; is that true?"

I hadn't a clue, all I knew was I was caring for a genius.

There were spells when he didn't paint, or try to; he'd be in better humour then, humming and smiling. I took him away at times like this to camp in my favourite places; that was when our loving was most perfect.

About a year on, there was a marathon silence. I suggested a trip; he just stared. I offered to pose for him; he sniggered and said: "Pose for the parish priest." One lovely May evening he asked the window, "Is the work of art about the world or about itself?"

And the next afternoon when I came home with groceries he was gone. His note said:

I thought you would be just passing through, now it seems that I was. I haven't found here what I needed.

I cried all night and all next day. Over four more days I nibbled through the food in the fridge, and wept, and slept in a chair. Then I rose in a trance one evening and began to dig a grave behind the house. At two feet I tired, and lay down, and slept. When I awoke, the sun was up. I felt new and strong. I decided to resume my work for women, but this time in the capital. No mere man would be allowed to shatter my life. I set off, singing, "I have crashed in your grave"; there was a line something like that in a poem.

I parked my car on Stephen's Green that afternoon and went

strolling; I ended up in a newsagent's in Talbot Street. A little 60 year-old man was causing a disturbance: reading aloud, talking to himself, laughing.

"I was at Pontius Pilate's house and pissed against it," he announced at one stage.

An assistant asked him to leave. As he reversed towards the door he held up a hand, protesting: "Peace, peace there in the belfry: service begins," and his parting shot was: "I live in hope to escape the rope."

I left half a minute after him. From the doorway I could see him 50 yards away, scurrying. Then the street exploded: cars, people, windows, earth, the little man, everything. I found myself stretched on the pavement with a severed foot on my chest.

The next thing I remember is running out of petrol and making out the word 'Dingle' on a signpost. The name captivated me and I set out to walk there, singing:

> *And the oul' triangle*
> *Goes Dingle dangle*
> *All along the banks*
> *Of the Royal Canal.*

And suddenly there *was* a canal; I hurried along it. The next signpost said 'Blennerville'; I crossed a bridge, rounded a corner, staggered, slipped, fell and vomited against the base of a gigantic ugly shell of a building. I lay there semiconscious for hours. At dawn I saw the building was a windmill, and I discovered that I'd lost my pilgrim's shell. I was too sick to rise.

My Good Samaritan was an elderly woman named Maggie Murphy; she brought me to her home in the Black Valley, one of the loveliest places in the country. I spent a week in bed, raving sometimes about parish priests and Pontius Pilate, crying a lot, and rubbing invisible stains off the sheets. I moped all through the summer, grieving for Robin, not wanting ever again to do anything. Until one evening, after a thunderstorm, Phil, Maggie's husband, strapped on his pipes and played slow airs. I had goosepimples. I was back in Winnie's kitchen, hearing her sing. Only this time I wanted to do likewise. I asked Phil to teach me, and a new life began. I gave hours every day to the music; I was never more alive than when least myself, lost in its magic. I never felt freer than when subjected to the tyranny of the tunes. And if Robin didn't cease to haunt me, he did move farther off.

Three years I spent in the Black Valley, not once venturing out. I helped Phil with the sheep, Maggie with housework, I learned bits of Spanish from their daughter Siobhán. At odd moments I'd savour and wonder about words: *miel, estrella, peregrino, lágrima, sangre, espejo, mirlo;* they described a world I knew, but they suggested as well another world just as real that would always evade my grasp.

On May Day 1977 Phil handed me his pipes and said, "You can go now."

And I did, in trepidation. I had no idea what I would do. I couldn't bring myself that night to enquire about bed and breakfast; I slept in the old Morris Minor.

I became, in time, the best-known unknown piper in the country. I played in tiny places almost always – poky village pubs and country kitchens. I never had a crowd of more than 50. I often played for ten, or two or three, and I was often happy playing for none at all. In my finest moments I became shy, as if overheard whispering to a lover. Yet I craved to be heard; I wanted to sprinkle music on every townland in Ireland. And my ally in this was – don't laugh – the old Telephone Directory, Part Two. The placenames were poetry, they were music, they were love-letters, smiles, invitations; a name on a page, like a face in a crowd, could start me on a starry-eyed journey . . . to Teeboy, Riverstick, Gurteenatarriff, Tomnalossett, Derrycoosh, Ballybacon, Jerusalem,

Tang, Noggus, Nicker, Pluck,Garryharry, Pollynoon, Nafferty, Lisatillister, Umerafree . . . In seven years I made no friends, I was never long enough in one place.

A rift opened up between me and the music. I didn't fall out of love with it, rather the reverse; it no longer gave me joy. I persevered, playing impersonally: if I were a perfect instrument playing another instrument, I hoped, I could still make perfect music. But my strings were stretched too tight.

In a pub in Enniskerry, a snuff-stained old priest grasped my hands and said: "By God, daughter, you're Christ's own piper!"

I burst into tears and sobbed for minutes. An elderly woman gave me a brandy, introduced herself as Doctor Longpass, and insisted on putting me up for the night. As we walked towards her house she kept repeating: "The best always happens."

I sleepwalked that night; I awoke trying to insert a car-key into a mirror. I sat on my bed then for hours, looking in a daze at my life. I was still there just before 8.00 when the birds became indignant, and the mirror swung like a pendulum, causing my face to vanish and reappear. A cloud of dust floated down from the ceiling and settled in my hair. I remembered Madam Joan, the fortune-teller, and decided to go home to Winnie. I left Doctor Longpass wondering if the insurance would cover a crack left in her gable by the earthquake.

I arrived in Dysart as Winnie was being buried. There were two dozen onlookers, no mourners. The priests were Father MacManamon and . . . Father James Costello. I couldn't stay in the cemetery; I got in the car and drove to Winnie's. I entered the house and was assailed by the smell of my teenage years. I sat down for a long time and remembered. I noticed a flamenco tape beside the cassette player. I played it and heard a man sing this: "*Teniendo el agua tan cerca, me estoy muriendo de sed*" – 'I'm right beside the water and still I'm dying of thirst.'

When he sang it the second time I wept, not for my own pain but for shame at my neglect of Winnie. I resolved to make amends by going back to my work for women; I would return the pipes to Phil Murphy.

For some reason I made a detour to Abbeyphelim, to confide my plans to Isobel Freeley. Eleven years had made a change in her: her eyes were darker and deeper. "You're running away," she said, before I had told her anything. "Your calling has become difficult, like lovemaking without love. It's your chance to love, for the first time perhaps, and, if needs be, to make reparation too." I found the convent's motto as puzzling as before.

I went back on the road, dispensing with the telephone directory, drifting as if blown by some wind. It was all work; the music resisted me. I felt permanently embarrassed, as though publicly feuding with a lover. I got no closer, personally, to my listeners than before. Playing, I was most often unaware of them, and now and again I forgot about myself: I didn't exist at such moments, I was the music. Was the music better then? Was it love? I have no idea. They were seven lean years.

Depression: that was what was wrong with me, this man told me; it was written all over me, he knew about such things. We were in a pub in Four Roads; his name was Hugh Fane, Aodh to his friends, He could cure me in a month, he said; he and his partner ran a recovery centre for people like me. He had an honest face and I was at the end of my tether; I put myself in his hands.

I followed his car through a maze of dark roads for an hour. His house, at the end of an avenue, was low and grim. Once inside, he took a large key from inside his trousers and locked the door. He showed me a pleasant room, told me I would meet his partner in the morning, and said goodnight. When he woke me for breakfast I saw that my windows were barred. Were there other patients, I asked. Not at the moment, I was told. He showed me round; *all* the windows were barred. In his study he introduced me to his partner: a life-size female bust on his desk, carved from dark wood, with small breasts and no arms; she was astonishingly beautiful. 'Nevertitty' he called her; she was the only woman who had ever shared his bed. A ladder led to a loft where he slept. The study floor was covered with piles of books; part of my therapy, I learned, would be to write critiques of two a week. I could play the pipes while he prepared meals or was out; I would not interrupt his reading or writing.

He appeared pleased with my first few critiques. He fed me well. He took me walking three days a week, by the lake in front of the house or in the forest behind it. He smiled a lot, naming trees, flowers, birds. Where were we, I asked him on our first walk, and where was my car? We were in a great, good place, he told me slowly, and my car was safe. That was the day he showed me his pistol: a beautiful thing, he called it, demonstrating its workings, a flawless work of art.

He was away on Saturdays, returning with provisions and books; these he presented to me gleefully, as so many gifts. Would the cure take long, I asked, after a month. Longer, he said. When I enquired again he affected not to hear; or he would say: "Would you agree that John Fowles is too clever to be good?" or "Can you make head or tail of this magic realism stuff?"

I sulked, failed to deliver my weekly quota; he forgot to invite me to meals. I wrote a new critique; I got smiles and lobster.

Months later I feigned illness; he saw through me. But I *was* ill: I couldn't look at the pipes, I stopped counting days, even Saturdays. I tried to lose myself in the books: *The Uses of Enchantment, The Manufacture of Madness, The Mirror in the Roadway, The Birds Fall Down, The Towers of Trebizond, By Grand Central Station I Sat Down and Wept, You are now Entering the Human Heart* . . . But my rage broke through; I became obsessed with stealing his pistol. On our walks I listened for engine noises; I heard a Boeing once. In desperation I looked to the pipes for a lifeline: I played whenever I could, though it was like eating broken glass.

I plodded into my second year, half aware. I nibbled at the mountain of books; every book tasted the same, and the mountain grew. In the autumn something in me collapsed. I wept and moped. Sleep was a jungle: I was snarled at, shrieked at, stung; I awoke gratefully to prison, jaded. Around Christmas I developed a fever. He looked after me: I remember linen changes, drinks, night watches. Afterwards there were no books for weeks. We walked every day, a little more each day. The forest seemed boundless, the lake was an ocean, we were the only people left in the world.

"I can't let you go, can't you see that?" he said, the day he set me reading again. *The Siren and the Seashell, Walking Naked, The Roundness of Eggs, The Mirror at Midnight, An Imagined Life, Flight from the Enchanter, At Play in the Fields of the Lord, A Ring Has No End* . . . and a hundred more. I grew calm, observing myself from a distance. Reading began to help me cope; I found myself liking books. And I lived for my piping, a necessary drug.

I showed more interest in my jailer. I responded more civilly to his questions. I grew curious about his piles of notes, his manuscripts, his huge waste-paper basket, his frustration. Why was he like this? Could he be helped? I began initiating conversations; he was taken aback, embarrassed. I put more thought into my critiques. I thought of him as my audience when piping, and tried to move him.

As I became more settled, he grew more restless. He paced his study floor for longer, night and day. He spent more time away, and came home with drink. "Play your pipes!" he would order at odd times, and have me play for an hour; "Shut that bloody racket!" he would occasionally shout when I tuned up at my standard time.

One evening I heard him snoring in his study. I peeped in: there was a whiskey bottle on the table, beside his pistol and his keys. I have never known such fear as at that moment. I looked at him for ages, then tiptoed to the kitchen and drank a pot of coffee. He snored all night and I heard every snore, my heart beating.

I found that the best thing for his nerves was a selection of slow airs. I'd go into a trance, put myself in Murphy's kitchen, and let Phil do the playing. It always worked, though never for very long.

One evening last April I found him stuffing papers in the range. He shouted at me: "I can't write! Do you understand? I want to write, I can't write, I have nothing to write: nothing to write about or from or with or for. I can't stand writing, I hate writing, and I *must* write! And I can't, do you understand?"

I stayed out of his way that night with my book, the title is on the tip of my tongue: it's hilarious until a little boy dies from the kick of a horse. I got no further. In the morning I found Nevertitty on the floor; my jailer lay at the edge of the loft, his head protruding, his eyes staring, his mouth dripping blood onto his partner.

I had to fish in his drawers for the keys. His car wouldn't start; the distributor cap was missing. I took my pipes and, being suddenly afraid of the avenue, I headed into the forest.

I forgot to bring food. It was raining. There was forest, then bog, then forest. Dark came, day came, dark. I walked, rested, walked, slept, wept. I sprained my left ankle; my pipes-case became a two-handed crutch. There was no human sight or sound. This place could not be on any map; I was abandoned on the arse of the earth. I couldn't remember my name; I was a character in a fiction or a dream.

On the third morning, at the edge of a forest, I came on a deserted house. There were scraps of bread on the ground. I limped towards them, and a lame dog appeared, snarling. I coaxed him, calling him Moses. I reached for a crust, and he snapped; I wrestled with him, and lost. And I fell, hurting my right knee. I abandoned the pipes and crawled into the forest. Then for comfort I turned, and rowed in slow motion along the clay. I sensed light, heard a cock crow, and quickened my pace. And landed upside down in a ditch. I passed out.

I awoke in the room I was born in. In a dressing-table mirror I could see Dysart chapel through the window beside my bed. I heard bees in the attic. I dozed, and heard a rustling. A crow stood on the dressing-table with a lump of clay in its beak. It bent its head to a saucer of water and rinsed; a gold ring emerged from the clay. The crow hopped and faced me; I shrank. It took off and swerved over me. I screamed. As it flew through the window I found the ring in my mouth. I awoke again, and saw a gold ring on my finger.

No one else was about. I walked to Winnie's. The house was dilapidated, the garden overgrown. And then it dawned on me: the place was mine; who else would Winnie have left it to? In the orchard I found a snow-white donkey: a two-year-old colt; I christened him Róisín. I untied him, mounted, and rode across the stepping-stones between a guard of honour of two magpies.

And I've been riding since, full of joy. I'm more beautiful than when I was sixteen, I'd kiss myself as readily as then. And no one refuses me a cup of water, or bread and a bed for the night. And no man has robbed my ring or affronted my honour. And in the dream-time between the ditch and the ring, I conceived: a mystery. I am four months with child. And my daughter will bring joy to me and to many: she may be a Mozart, she may be mentally retarded, the difference is slight, she'll be a wonder.

As I journey I sense a presence at my back; at any moment I could be overtaken by . . . glory. Róisín could sprout black wings and sing and fly; I could find my precious stone, my pilgrim shell; I might hear my pipes beckon me with magic music, and play

unearthly music when we meet. I might see a stone boat sail up the
Shannon and unload a cargo of wonders in Clonmacnoise . . .
The wonderful is the norm. The best way to say 'I don't know,'
is 'I wonder,' and the best form of 'maybe,' is 'we'll see'. We will.
Father Mac tried to frighten Dysart once with a sermon about
death, and he said something he said God said in the Bible: "I will
show you fear in a handful of dust."

But that's not what God said; somebody took it down wrong.
What God said was: "I will show you joy in a handful of dust."

*I felt special in childhood too, without omens or talismans or
wonders; I didn't even have a river. I had no mentor. I had two
antagonists, whom I wasn't lucky enough to see dead before I
spread my wings.*

*Joy weighs up action, contemplation, love and art before her
first collapse. (The severed foot is her own foot, off the accelerator.)
She then progresses through rest, art, work, depression, prison,
exhaustion, abandonment, insanity. This is my life.*

*As a student, I had a synthesis in my head: art could be work,
executed in love, for love. And work could be art, blah blah, blah
blah. As a young teacher, I was full of ideals. I tried to write as
well, but the well was dry, there was no well. And a couple of
nervous breakdowns saw to the ideals. In my late twenties I
developed my philosophy of pointlessness: everything I did had
to be as pointless, as useless as possible. I worked hard to apply
this to the classroom, but found myself continually frustrated. A
third breakdown took me out of teaching, and I metamorphosed
into a placenames specialist; pointlessness became attainable,
instantly, eminently, permanently.*

*What do I know of prison? I have been in the same job for
fifteen years, the same marriage for twelve, the same carcass for
47; I had the same parents for 33. As Samuel Beckett wrote to*

me the other day – what a lift his card was! – 'Time is long, space is short, and in the tomb we have no room to fart.'

My view too.

Hugh Fane, jailer, failure: the key to his literary sterility is in his drawers: he's impotent. He sees his pistol as 'a flawless work of art': is that possible? A good subject for a debate. I would say yes. I would also say no.

My father bullied me into learning the uileann pipes; I played incorrigibly badly until he backed off. I suppose I was emulating him when I put Joy through the wringer. She's good, perhaps she will play, in time to come, unearthly music.

A niggling question: is she overcome at the end by insanity or by insight? Could a mad woman tell that story?

Yours candidly,

Enda Ring.

Dear . . . dear . . . dear Danny's granny,

That's the best I can do; I can't remember your name, though I heard it once or twice that summer. My new playmates – great fans of your jam sandwiches – called you only 'Danny's granny'. Danny's mammy, he informed me early on, was your daughter, Chrissie; his daddy only God and Chrissie knew. I couldn't parse that, but, unwilling, at seven, to risk a ten-year-old's scorn, I said nothing. His grandad had, as he put it, 'fecked off t'England' some years before, and had not been heard of since.

   Your deserted status, I am impressed to recall, made you feel neither embittered nor inferior. As supplier of flowers for the local church, you enjoyed the compliments you received on your special feast-day displays. I got caught for the rosary in your house once; the trimmings contained prayers for 'Daddy's welfare, spiritual and material, and his speedy return home' as well as for 'the conversion of the lapsed of the parish'. Danny informed me that these were the people to whom you had him deliver old copies of the Blessed Martin Magazine, The Word *and* The Far East.

   I went with him on his next such visit; it was the last day of my holiday. The subject of our mission was a family recently moved over from England: a taciturn local man, his weary-looking English wife, and their gawky eight-year-old son; they had never been seen in church. I remember the awkwardness. We said who we were, handed over the magazines and drank warm lemonade. As we got up to leave, the man asked Danny if his grandfather's name was Lukie. Danny said yes, and added that he had fecked off t'England. The man said: 'Sure I know the bollocks well. Isn't he livin' beyond in Coventry with the mistress of a whorehouse? Spongin' off her he is.' The woman hooshed us out.

I didn't understand our silence on the way back to your house, and as soon as we met you I repeated what the man had said, stumbling over the words that were new to me. Danny kicked my ankle, and your smile went AWOL. But only for a while: by the time I set off to my auntie's it was at its post again, resplendent as ever.

That was the last time I saw you. I returned home next day; my auntie sold up and moved, and I never went back there for holidays. But your kindness stayed with me, and your dignity, and your smile.

I think I know the rest of your story. You persevered praying for Daddy's speedy return, putting a different twist on the meaning of the word as the years passed. You held your head as erect in church as any lily you placed there. You probably helped Christine rear one or two more fatherless children. You lavished jam sandwiches on another generation. And no doubt you didn't neglect the lapsed of the parish.

Could I trouble you with a story? You are nothing if not patient, and the shrink says I'm better to be telling my yarns to others than to have them buzzing around in my head.

Back in 1952, when I was twenty years of age, I fell in love with a prostitute.

I was already driving a cab, and I was asked to pick up a

customer at this big secluded house in Rathgar. When the door opened, I saw this young one chatting to a man who was leaving, and I'd never seen the likes of her; she was slim and tanned, she had a beautiful smile and lovely short auburn hair. I had her in my sights for only twenty seconds, because your man closed the door. I drove him to Merrion Square, and he asked me to do the full run to Rathgar and back twice a week. I did that for a month or so, and waited while he did his business, but I never got another look at the girl. Then I heard the place was the highest-class brothel in Dublin. I was livid: the thought of that creature being manhandled sickened my stomach. I ambushed her that night as she left the place, and told her I wanted to marry her and take her out of there. I had no intention of saying that, but when I heard myself I knew I meant it. And I didn't even know her shagging name!

She told me to go home to my mammy.

I stood your man up after that. I became obsessed with the girl; I dreamt of kidnapping her; I saw us rearing half a dozen kids in some uncorrupted place. I ambushed her again and got nowhere. Then I paid my money and got to see her in her room; I begged her to let me support her. She told me what she earned and told me to keep my ice-cream money; she was supporting her mother and five younger brothers and sisters. I asked her how long more she would have to keep it up, and she said three or four years. Could I see her in the meantime, I asked her. Yes, she said, provided I didn't talk about her work. And she gave me half a smile. Una her name was, Una Kilfeather, and she was two years older than me. She lived in Phibsboro and her mother thought she worked for a doctor.

The following Sunday I took her for a drive. She told me she had a five year old son, Liam; she said nothing about the father and I bit my tongue. I tried to kiss her when I left her home. She wouldn't let me: no kissing till she'd quit the job. Jesus! Four years without a kiss! A mark of respect for me, she said; I could give her a brief hug on saying goodnight. Jasus, she sounded like a Franciscan. And she was enjoying it.

We took a drive and a walk every Sunday, nearly always in the county Wicklow. We brought Liam the odd time. My mother gave me an Irish setter for my twenty-first birthday and he came along then too. Cockles I called him , me being muscles. Una let me hold her hand on our walks, and I used to try to send my brain into my fingers to get the full feel of it.

We were going out about six months when I decided to chance my arm. I asked her would she marry me when she gave up her work. We were sitting on the banks of the Dargle in Knocksink Wood. I remember it well: Cockles was going mad in the water; he'd been chasing a butterfly for ages, and was just after spotting an otter; he was ploughing around like a lunatic and barking his head off; I could hardly hear myself.

"Ah, Christy, you're as bad as poor oul' Cockles there," says she. "Can you not take one thing at a time? It's far too soon to be talking about what might happen in three years' time." The stomach nearly fell out of me. I said nothing, but I couldn't sleep that night: if I was Cockles, she could be the bleeding otter, that would play at your feet and then slip away into the river. I called on her at her workplace next day.

" I want you to promise you'll marry me," I told her.

"Christy," says she, "can't you leave the future alone? Why do you want everything tied up?"

"Will you marry me, Una, yes or no?" says I.

"Maybe I will, maybe I won't," says she. "Who knows what'll happen?"

"Una," says I, "if you ever tell me you won't marry me, I'll do myself in."

"You will in your arse," says she.

There was a scissors on her dressing-table and I grabbed it, and I shoved the narrow leg of it through my shirt. The next thing there was blood everywhere and I was in a heap on the floor. I fainted, and woke up in Mount Carmel Hospital.

I wasn't there long; there was no serious damage done, but I felt bleeding stupid. Una came to see me every evening. I thought she was just mollycoddling me till I got better and that then she'd dump me. But one evening she said: "Christy, I *will* marry you. And I have my engagement ring here; it was my mother's."

She let me kiss her on the cheek.

"You'll put it on me when you get out," says she. "And I'll never wear it at work. I'll have the bloodstain on the carpet there to make me think of you; we couldn't get it out completely."

The following Sunday she brought me to her local church, St Peter's, and I put the ring on her finger in front of a statue of Our Lady, and she kissed me on the lips.

"Just this once," says she; "exceptional circumstances."

We were two years engaged when she began to get hassle from your man, – the customer I used to bring to her. I won't tell you his name – and the one he gave me was false – but he ended up very high up after. Anyway, he wanted to set her up in a flat in Ballsbridge and have her all to himself. She told him she'd consider it when she was 60. He started showering her with presents, and he had her spied on.

One Thursday night I was having a jar and these two heavies told me there were great jobs for cabbies in England: I could get 500 of a handshake if I got out of the country within a fortnight, leaving no forwarding address. I tracked down your man the next day and told him the Long Fellow would hear about him if he didn't lay off: my father was in Boland's Mills in 1916, I said, and Dev had a great regard for our family. On the Saturday my brakes failed on the hill between Christchurch and the river; I could have bleeding killed someone: the car had been tampered with during the night.

But it was Una who put a stop to the whole caper; she informed me on Monday night that we'd be hearing no more from your man. What did she say to him, I asked her. And do you know what she said to him? She waited till he had his way with her, and when she had him there beside her heaving like a spent salmon she says to him: "Do you see them scissors?" says she. That's what she said to him; that's all it took. And when she told me that, she kissed me: the first right kiss I got in my fecking life. And she was quitting the job straight away; she had decided her family were well enough looked after. Besides, says she, my bloodstain was gone, from all the people trooping in and out. We were going to be married in three months.

As it happened, my older brother, Alfie, was due to get married soon as well, and we arranged for a double wedding. A week or so before the big day, he invited me out for a jar, and he said something I never forgot; he said: "One of the things I'm looking forward to is this: I'll have kids, and they'll have kids, and their kids will have kids, and so on, and in a thousand years there could be a million people of every colour walking up and down the world with my blood in them."

Outside the pub afterwards, we were congratulating ourselves and one another; we were fairly jarred. I said something about Una's toughness and her sense of humour.

"Yeah," says he, "and she's great in bed as well."

Well, I flattened him with a belt in the snot that Henry Cooper would have been proud of, and I walked away and left him lying there with his nose pumping blood into the gutter. I felt a bit bad about that after, because he fell under a bus the next day and was made mincemeat of. I wondered if maybe I'd made him groggy, but I said nothing. I realised that life doesn't give a shite about the individual, only the species.

We postponed the wedding of course, and we got married the time of the carry-on in Hungary and the Suez Canal. With all the formalities, Una found out that my name wasn't Christopher, like I had her thinking, but Eucharisticus, on account of the Congress the year I was born. She nearly wet herself laughing and promised she'd tell no-one until I deserved it. We got a house across the street from my mother, and Liam, of course, moved in with us as well.

Straight away I made my first discovery about married life: it's very different from single life. I don't just mean sex, I mean *living* with someone. I couldn't get used to being with Una so much, and I loved it. We spent half our time laughing.

We were six months married, and Una was just pregnant, when this bloke I hardly knew says to me in a pub: "Did you ever hear of a geezer called Gogarty?" says he. "Oliver St John Gogarty. A great poet. He wrote a great poem about this place; I must show it to you the next time I see you."

And he did show me a poem: the first two lines were:

> *I will live in Ringsend*
> *With a red-headed whore . . .*

When I showed it to Una she said: "We're moving. You're going to Galway tomorrow to buy a house."

Two days later I put a deposit on a house near the University, and we moved in the day they let the first dog loose in space.

Peter was born that Christmas, and before I knew where I was we had five more: Phelim, Paula, Deirdre, Tracy and Donal. And fairly soon I made my second discovery: when you've children things speed up: there's lots more happening around you: noise, rows, clutter, breakages, ailments . . . Una was well able for it all, in fact she revelled in it, she was like your man what's-his-name Yeltsin conducting the German band when he was pissed. I wasn't so patient: many's the time, after a hard day, I'd hoosh the bloody lot of them out of the house, or I'd take Cockles for a walk and tell him my troubles. That's when I could get the fecker to listen to me: most of the time he'd be rooting in the neighbours' flowerbeds. Una was the only one that dog would be quiet for.

To be fair to me though, I wasn't completely useless with the children. I was good at making up yarns: *The Magic Scissors, The Man Who Wasn't Famous, The Mystery-Solving Dog, The First Taxi in Space* . . . I used to tell Una stories too. She'd snuggle up to me in bed and say, "Tell us a story." And I'd tell her one, one of the ones I was after telling the youngsters. Often she'd be asleep before it was over, but I'd go on to the end anyway, and then I'd tell her she was the finest fecking woman in the world, and I'd say I was sorry for being good for nothing only driving a bloody car. I came up with another game too: I'd let on she used to talk in her sleep, and I'd tell her the things I heard from her, *moryah*, the night before: "The woman in the Credit Union said I have only 60 short red hairs in my account" or: "There's a lily growing out of my fanny and it's trying to play *Roddy McCorley*", or: "Take that dog out of the fridge or you'll wear a black dress for your First Communion." We used to nearly rupture ourselves laughing and try to work out what dreams they belonged to.

I'd often lie awake at night and imagine the house was a taxi, travelling down the road of time, and I was the driver, carrying VIPs through dangerous traffic. Or I was a ship's captain, steering by the moon and stars while all the crew and passengers were asleep. I was proud – and humble at the same time, if you know what I mean – to be the head of a family: it was the only real responsibility in the world.

We had a bit of a falling out, myself and Una, the time Donal, the youngest lad, was born. Cockles died the same day, and we were as sorry as we could be in the circumstances; I mean he'd been with us for thirteen years. I went and got him stuffed, and Una wasn't one bit pleased.

"Let the living bury their dead," says she. "How do you think I could bear to be looking at him for the rest of my life? Out he's going."

"Over my dead body," says I, and I was never as cross in my life. We had a truce for a few days, with Cockles standing guard beside my rocking-chair. But then I had to go into hospital with my appendix, and when I came home again there was no sign of the bugger. I said nothing, because Donal was giving Una a lot of trouble, and she said nothing either. And would you believe this? That dog was never again mentioned – not as much as his bloody name. And do you know something else? Something went out of our marriage. We had no more stories in bed.

In the 70s we had a houseful of teenagers, and I made my third discovery: when your kids think they're smarter than you are, they're often right. (I wouldn't *say* that to them though.) I couldn't handle the growing-up stuff at all, I wasn't able to argue with them, I left that to Una. But on one point I couldn't be budged: I couldn't give a damn what they wanted to work at, but once a youngster reached sixteen, I wanted him or her to show a serious interest in *something*. Liam had set a great example years before. He went to work in the library at eighteen, but for years before that he was studying the growth of Galway city, tracing the history of every bleeding shop and commercial premises; sure isn't he the recognised authority on the subject? (I often wonder if his father was a scholar; Una told him who he was when he was fifteen, but I was never told.)

I had great hopes for Peter, and he let me down. I was terrible fond of him and he was a likeable young lad, but you never saw such a butterfly in your bleeding life; one week he'd be building a radio, the next week he'd be putting a telescope together, or writing poems, or taking photographs, or learning to play the guitar or make candles; he could stick at nothing. I warned him often enough, and when he got a disgraceful Leaving Cert result I lost the head: I told him he was a good-for-nothing pup and he needn't expect to board much longer in my kennel. Sure I didn't mean it at all, but the next day he disappeared, leaving a note stuck on my windscreen: just eight words written out in three lines:

> *Elsewhere is air*
> *for birdsong and*
> *burgeoning pear.*

"What the fuck does that mean?" says I to Una.

"It means," says she, "that you're poisoning him with your bad breath. You're after driving away your firstborn with your foul mouth, may God forgive you. And you needn't expect him back soon; don't you know how sensitive he is? Let them live their lives, can't you, let them make their mistakes. I've a good mind to tell them your name."

He sent her a card from London within the week, and many another card after, but there never was an address, and he never asked after me.

Phelim did his Inter the same year and took summer work with a man that had horses in Bushypark. At the end of the holidays he announced that he was staying on; he was finished with school. That was fine by me. He's managing a stud farm in Meath now and has shares in a couple of horses; he's the best off of the lot of them.

The three girls were a bit on the wild side. I wasn't worried about them, though; I knew they were dead sound, they were very keen on their books. Donal, at the time I'm talking about, was too young to give trouble, and he was as good at fixing things as at breaking them.

In 1977 I got some kind of an itch: I began to wonder if I was capable – psychologically, I mean – of being unfaithful to Una. Things hadn't been great between us since Peter left, and there was this waitress I liked the look of, that I often drove out to Barna after her work: a fine plump woman of 35 with shiny black hair and a gamey glint in her eye. I decided to test myself, and one Thursday evening in November – the 17th, I remember it well – I got myself invited into her bedsit. She plonked down on the bed and peeled off her right stocking, and Jasus, what did I see only six toes on her foot. I was out the door as quick as if she had a cloven hoof. End of experiment, I'm telling you.

Phelim's twenty-first birthday was on Una's fiftieth, in 1980. He mentioned that there was a horse named Una running that day in some little place in England at twenty to one. I put on 50 quid and gave her a thousand that evening. She didn't give a shite about money really, but things improved a bit between us.

The following year we had our twenty-fifth anniversary, and that was the day I missed Peter most. I said nothing, but Una knew, and she brought me to the bedroom after the dinner and put her arms around me and told me I was a good father. That evening Donal started telling us that that there was no heaven and no God. I was going to put manners on him but one look from Una changed my mind. He turned out a fine young fellow after. He works in a dental laboratory now and plays harmonica with a jazz band.

Paula qualified as a nurse that same year, and started going out with a gynaecologist. I didn't like him much, I thought he was too sweet to be wholesome, and I was glad when they broke up after a year. I wasn't too pleased, though, when she headed off to Australia, but Una produced a bottle of champagne and said that in future we'd celebrate every ship that we launched.

Deirdre went off that year as well, to Freiburg, to improve her German, and fell in love with an actor. And it was about this time I made my fourth discovery; 'tis when you think you have them reared that things really begin to happen. She returned to Freiburg after her BA in '84, and in no time she was married to your man: a registry office job. Her daughter, Melanie, was born in '85, our first grandchild. And Tracy qualified that summer too, as a lab technician, and got a job in Kerry.

Poor Tracy, my favourite, the spit of her mother. She was drowned in a sailing accident on a dirty black Friday in May '86.

She wouldn't be buried yet if it depended on me: I was helpless; Liam made all the arrangements. When we got the house to ourselves again on the Tuesday, Una put a bottle of champagne on the table. I was speechless, but she opened it; we cried and we drank. We were barely finished when a postcard came through the letterbox: "Spreading my wings this weekend and heading out to sea. Love, Tracy." There was a picture of a boat with white sails, and seagulls wheeling round it.

Paula came home that October; she was five months pregnant. I could handle that.

"Who's the father?" I asked her the first evening.

"He's a chef," says she, "his name is Eddie Goolagong."

"Oh, Jesus!" says I, "he's black!"

"Very," says she.

I said nothing, only got up; I looked around for a second for Cockles, the Lord have mercy on him, and I went out for a long walk.

Una didn't speak to me that night, but the next day she told me she had done two things: she'd persuaded Paula to stay on and have her baby in Galway, and she'd emptied her Credit Union account to send Eddie his fare over. I didn't talk to either of them for a week, and I found myself wishing that that waitress had only ten toes.

I was still sulking at Hallowe'en when I attended a benefit concert for an injured driver. I was actually enjoying it towards the end, and then Paula's name was announced. It hadn't occurred to me that she'd be asked to play, though she was the only real musician in the family; Donal didn't compare. She clambered onto the stage with her concertina, and played. The lovely gentle rhythms I remembered from years before, they brought the tears to my eyes. She was so composed . . . Her hands were moving no more than if she was knitting, and her body swaying just that little bit, as if every tune was a lullaby; as if she was playing for her child. And then the idea hit me that she *was*

68

knitting: knitting a christening shawl of lovely notes, and they were falling on us all like gentle rainbow-coloured flakes of snow. And that's why I was ready to welcome Eddie at Christmas. A nicer guy you couldn't meet, and he didn't mind me at all calling him Snow-White.

The baby arrived on Valentine's Day and they called him Christopher, after me. Christy Goolagong, my first and only grandson. Christy Goolagong: I was so proud to repeat it, and I was heartbroken when they left for Perth on Patrick's Day. They got married down under soon after.

Una spent the next two Christmases in hospital with pneumonia; the second time she agreed to give up the fags. Deirdre came home that time too to look after her; the young one, Melanie, was a great comfort to Una, but Deirdre wasn't herself. Eventually she told Una her story, and Una told it to me. A couple of years earlier, her actor had turned into an actress: Hans became Greta, and continued to act with the same company. And stayed on in the apartment with Deirdre: they couldn't afford a second one. It got better: the previous year Greta had installed a girlfriend – a frigging *girlfriend* – in the apartment, and before long little Melanie was calling all three of them Mutti. Deirdre was going to file for a divorce and move to Bamberg.

My blood was boiling as I was listening to all this funny stuff, and when I'd heard it all I rang a travel agency. Una took the phone out of my hand and asked me what I thought I was doing.

"I'm flying to Germany," says I, "and I'm going to kick the arse off that Hansel and Gretel fellow, by Jesus I am!"

Well, she laughed till I thought she'd choke, and she got me laughing too; it was better than the old days, and you'd never guess we had a daughter whose life was unbelievably fucked up. But, as Una said, for some illnesses the patient is the only doctor, and sure enough, Deirdre has it all sorted out by now.

We took our first foreign holiday that summer, in the Canaries. It did her good, but as the year wore on her shortness of breath was terrifying. She insisted we spend Christmas in Phibsboro with her mother, still going strong at 82. We attended midnight Mass in St Peter's, and she kissed me in front of our statue. After the dinner she says to me: "See if you can look him up in the new year." Peter she was talking about. We knew he was OK from the cards that still came from London, but there never was a clue as to where he lived or worked. It was hard to think of him imagining, for example, that Tracy was still alive. Her death was the great wound in my life, but him being lost was another. Bamberg and Perth were much nearer to me than London. It made me sad to hear birds singing, and I couldn't look at a pear.

On Stephen's Day she asked me to cut her toenails: it was a job she always hated. I did it, and she put her arms around me and says she: "You're a bit of a gobshite, Christy Kane, but you were always a dab hand with the scissors, and if I had to live my life again, you're the man I'd pick to live it with."

She took bad two days before New Year's Eve, and her mother's GP got her into Mount Carmel Hospital; she was put in the very ward I was in 35 years before: number 104. She slept a lot, and spoke very little.

"Christy," says she to me on the Saturday, "I won't be far away from you."

It took me a while to cop on that she was talking about dying. I told her I'd have her home in three weeks' time.

"I'm banjaxed," says she.

"Don't be stupid," says I.

"I'm bollixed," says she.

On New Year's Day, in the evening, I went to see her. She was asleep and she did look bad right enough: her face was purple, her mouth was open, her cheeks were hollow, her breath was coming and going in little puffs; only for her hair I'd have hardly known her. She woke eventually and asked me the time.

"Ten," says I.

"Morning or night?" says she.

"Night," says I.

"What day is it?"

"Monday."

"There'll be only one more Tuesday and Wednesday," says she.

The old bush telegraph got working. The three lads came and went. Deirdre turned up; even Paula flew in. Relations came, and old friends. I don't know how many priests gave her absolution or where the hell they came out of. She clasped everyone's hand and nodded, until she sank into a coma around two on the Wednesday. An old nun came in and sat by the window, knitting.

"I'm Sister Madeleine," says she to me. "I'm a Blue Nun. I live in Mount Carmel Hospital, in Dublin."

"Gaga," says I to myself.

But the next thing she said pulled me up: "I just sit here and watch them go."

And she sat there knitting, some class of a garment with a pile of colours.

On Thursday around noon I said I wanted Una to myself for a while. I cleared the ward: Liam, Paula, Phelim, a nurse, a priest, all out. I didn't bother the old nun, she was hardly there.

I talked to Una. I said sorry for hounding Peter. I reminded her of our Wicklow walks, and the stories I used to tell her in bed. And I admitted that I never heard her talking in her sleep.

"I *will* find Peter," I said, "I will," and I thought I saw her nodding. And out of the blue I told her I'd have cheated on her once only for the woman had two toes too many.

"I know," says she.

"How?" says I.

"You talked in your sleep," says she.

And then she said my name – my real name, I mean, Eucharisticus – and she chuckled; she fucking chuckled, as much as to say: "You're a fucking eejit." And 'twas only then it hit me: she was after *talking*! After twenty-two hours in a coma the woman was after *speaking*! I got excited, but she didn't say another word. I kept talking: I thanked her for loving me and rearing the children, and I said that if I lived a million years I'd never find anyone like her, my own little auburn-haired beauty. And then I started to sing, as softly as I could, the song we used to sing beside the Dargle:

> *In Dublin's fair city*
> *Where the girls are so pretty*
> *I first set my eyes*
> *On sweet Molly Malone . . .*

When I got to the chorus, a second voice joined in; it was the old nun at the window. I was in bits by the end of the second verse, and I let her sing the third on her own:

> *She died of a fever*
> *And no-one could save her,*
> *And that was the end*
> *Of sweet Molly Malone.*
> *But her ghost wheels her barrow*
> *Through streets broad and narrow,*
> *Crying: "Cockles and mussels*
> *Alive, alive-o!"*

By the time she got to the end I was crying like a baby into the bedclothes. She took me by the arm and said: "Why don't we go down to the kitchen, young man, and I'll make you a cup of tea."

At four o' clock Una's breathing got very heavy. Everyone knelt down, including the nun with the knitting; a nurse gave out the Rosary. At ten past there was a rattle, and then peace, as if a bird was after flying from a cage.

I'll spare you the details of the funeral. I got through it thanks to one sentence: *I am the resurrection and the life.* From the family gathering after, I'll give you just a couple of items.

I went to go to the toilet. Donal was inside, singing, *singing*:

> *Them bones, them bones, them dry bones . . .*

I was horrified: what class of a pagan was I after rearing at all, to be carrying on like that and his mother not cold in her grave? And then he was having a go at a Beatles song:

> *Blackbird singing in the dead of night,*
> *Take these broken wings and learn to fly:*
> *You were only waiting for this moment to arise.*

If he was half his age, I'd have burst in and given him a clip on the ear. And then I heard a sigh, and then a sniffle, and then a sob, and the poor little bastard was in floods of tears. I tiptoed away and emptied my tank in the garden.

Phelim joined me.

"Do you remember," says he, "the thousand quid you won on that horse called Una?"

"Why wouldn't I?" says I.

"Well," says he, "I didn't back her myself; I thought she hadn't an earthly. But I borrowed a grand belonging to the boss unknown to him the same day, and I put it on another horse that lost. I'd have been rightly in the shit only Ma gave me the thousand you gave her half an hour before."

"And did you ever give it back to her?" I asked him.

"Oh, I did," says he; "where else do you think she got the money to fly Eddie over the Christmas before young Christy was born? Sure Ma never had a bob in the Credit Union."

Well, actually she had £7.62 at the time of her death; they paid me twice that amount, as is their custom, when I went to close the account.

Paula wanted to bring me to Perth to enjoy their summer, but I wanted to face the empty house straight away. I wouldn't hear of moving in with any of the lads. Deirdre would have liked to stay, but she had to return immediately to Bamberg: she'd left Melanie with her new man. They were to marry shortly and move to Berlin: she wanted to be a writer, and with the wall down it seems that was the place to be. She told me later that throughout the whole journey to their new abode, Melanie kept chanting the two words, "Nana" and "Berlin".

I faced the empty house. Only it wasn't empty. She was like Molly Malone: her ghost wheeled her barrow through rooms broad and narrow. I pottered around, making tea, washing clean cups, opening wardrobes and tins. I found a tiny Christmas cake she made for the two of us before we went to her mother's: the last thing she ever baked. I dithered about it, then I washed it down with a mug of tea.

Sleeping in our bed was the hardest thing, but I did it, from the first night. And one night I wondered if there was anything in the lockers: there was one on either side but they were always locked. I rummaged in Una's handbag and found keys; one of them opened her locker. And inside, covered with black dust, was a folder with two hundred pages in her handwriting. The first page said: *Memoirs of a Red-Headed Whore,* and, underneath that, *To be published in its entirety or not at all.*

I sat on the bed and read the whole bloody thing in one go. It was one hell of a read. I had browsed through some old *Capuchin Annuals* of the fifties a few weeks before, and seen reference to several pillars of Catholic Ireland; well, a fair few of them were turning up again here. Oh, there was the odd Protestant pillar too; one of them, an Irish language enthusiast, for reasons she couldn't understand, nor me either, used to call her "knee-knock Una". There was never anything wrong with Una's knees.

I was wondering the whole way through whether I'd ask Liam to get it published when all those named were dead. The final paragraph decided me:

I married Christy for three reasons. First, I tested him hard, and he passed the tests; he proved he loves me. Second, there was an impulsive, unstable side to him; I was afraid he might do himself harm and I decided he needed looking after. And third, I love him deeply, and you don't have to give reasons for that.

No way was I going to have that made public. I brought the folder downstairs at six in the morning and opened the door of the range. But I couldn't do it, I couldn't destroy a thing that was like a cloth she wove from her memories while she was expecting our first child. And then I had a brainwave: I would take it to my grave; Liam would place it in my coffin, and leave a copy to the National Library in his will. Within a few days it was arranged.

My head was so full of the *Memoirs* that I forgot the other locker for two days. The same key opened it. All I could see at first was cobwebs, and then I pulled this thing towards me. It was Cockles. I had to sit down; I thought I'd have a heart attack. After a while I started to clean him, and I kept rubbing at him for ages and crying. I was at that for maybe an hour, in a kind of trance, until a noise brought me back. I wondered how he'd look beside my rocking-chair, but no; how could I bear to be looking at him for the rest of my life? I heard the noise again; it was the bin-lorry. I carried Cockles down the stairs like a sick child. At the gate I fondled his ears and kissed the top of his head. And when the lorry was just past the gate I let him go. For one eternal second he sailed through the air like in the old days. I turned away before I could see him mangled.

In June I went to London. I had no plan, except to come home in three weeks; I left the bright ideas department in Una's hands. I did the touristy things, and I enjoyed myself up to a point. For twenty days nothing happened. On the twenty-first I went into a church; I'm damned if I can remember the name of it. On the walls there were plaques to the memory of actors; many's the one of them I'd watched on the silver screen. One woman's epitaph took my fancy: *She served God right merrily.*

That was Una, I said to myself; if God is other people, that's exactly what she did. And there was this other one I liked: *Inspired player of small parts,*

and I wished to Jesus that could be said of me. I made for the door thinking those two phrases would be all I'd be bringing home. I stumbled into the sunlight, and I nearly knocked Peter off the footpath. He backed away and went as white as a sheet.

"Your mother is dead," I said to him.

He covered his face with his hands: a 33 year old man in a suit, but I was looking at an eighteen-year-old boy in a teeshirt, at a six-month-old baby with a bib. I said: "I'm sorry, son; forgive me. Forgive your stupid, stubborn, pigheaded thick of a father. I love you, Peter."

And he did forgive me. In the middle of London our own little Berlin wall came down. We talked and laughed for hours, and a few tears were shed. I stayed another fortnight. I phoned all the others with the good news, and Peter spoke to them for the first time in fifteen years. We planned a big reunion for Christmas. I nearly forgot to ask Peter what he worked at: he was with the British Museum, as a carbon-dating expert in the antiquities section.

The last five years have been bittersweet. We've had our reunions. I've holidayed in Perth and Berlin. But how could I not miss Una, more than I'd miss an amputated limb? Without her I'm not even half a man.

Deirdre has another daughter, Martha, and she published a book of short stories last year, in German. She says she's glad I can't read them; they must be desperate, or she must think I'm shocking innocent. There are two more little Goolagongs walking up and down the world – Geraldine and Oscar – and the great thing is that they're going walkabout in Galway. Yes, Paula and Eddie moved back to live with me three months ago. Paula is doing part-time work with special kids, and Eddie is about to open a restaurant in Wood Quay.

There's hullabaloo in the house and I love it. Well, sometimes. And I'm learning my last lesson about marriage: when you think you've finished with it, you find yourself back where you started.

The other great news is that the four lads are getting married next year: Donal, at 30, to a doctor from Limerick; Phelim, at 37, to a farmer from Carlow; Peter, at 39, to a teacher from Bangla Desh; and Liam, at 49, to a librarian from down the road. And it'll be four separate weddings, four days out. I'm 63; I hope to live to 93 and watch lots of little Kanes and Goolagongs and Fleischmanns carrying my blood around the globe. You know, poor Alfie, God be good to him, he was dead right after all: the species might be number one, but the individual, if he gets a lucky punch in, can make one hell of a mark.

Your husband 'fecked off t'England', Christy lost a son to London; that's why I picked you for this story. Worse, of course, Christy lost a child altogether. Sympathy aside, though, I'm not fond of the man. He reminds me of my father, who, despite more education, was the same sort of bombastic old bollocks. For starters, he – Christy – is a killer: he never faces what he did to his brother. That's the meaning of the contents of the lockers. Una's memoirs are truth, and he can't handle that, he buries it. And the stuffed and cobwebbed dog is the guilty secret – like a stubborn lump of bloody phlegm that suddenly, disgustingly comes up – and all he can do with that is have it minced. Cobwebs: notice how Christy has a thing about weaving and covering up: Paula's concertina notes are knitting a christening shawl, the old nun is knitting some class of a garment, Una's book is woven from her memories. Covering, cloaking, that's what's going on. And all that buzzing round, to stop him thinking.

He refers at one stage to 'the first dog let loose in space'. Never, of course, was dog less loose than Laika, but Eucharisticus had a sound intuition there: as a man called Camus wrote to me the other day: 'You can be as confined as you like in a life, and yet be a danger to the cosmos.' Mind you, Camus meant me – so he won't be blowing the froth off a pint of mine again in a hurry – but I see his words hitting old Christy on the head. No, I don't like the man.

Yours affectionately,

Enda Ring.

PREACHER

Dear Father Ball,

You don't know me, but I remember you well. I was the one who had you committed, or at least the one who reported you. Allow me to remind you of the episode.

I had no interest in the vocations' seminar, I went to oblige the Head and make up the numbers; five fellows and seven girls wasn't a bad attendance. Your talk was the one I most felt like skipping: I mean, look at the title, 'Giving up Everything for God', what a turn-on! Anyway, there you were, telling us the only real way to serve God was to live like angels, soaring above the desires of the flesh, when the class know-all, Clara Hughes, asked you what about the parents of the Little Flower, who had eight children. 'Five of whom became nuns,' you answered quickly. 'In fact they themselves had both wished to enter the religious life, and turned to matrimony only when that proved impossible. And there's something else' – here you lowered your voice – 'something that's not generally known: those eight children were not conceived in the usual manner. A needle was used to extract the . . . ah . . . the sperm from Louis and inject it into Zélie, to ensure that they would not experience pleasure, but pain.' Well, even at seventeen we knew enough to know you were sitting on your mouth at that stage, and the session broke up in hilarity. I was the one deputed to tell the Head, and before the day was out the word was that you were in the psychiatric unit of the local hospital. One of the lads, Joe Fannin, had a cousin working in the place, and he reported to us that you spent your time wanking in a private ward.

Interned for heresy you were, one might say. And yet, Father Ball, off the wall and all as you were, your notions epitomise for me an important strand in the weave of the Catholicism I know. That's a truism, of course, but none the less true for that. And so I wasn't that surprised when, a few years back, I saw posters around town announcing a mission to be preached by, among others, Father Robert Ball; you had been rehabilitated. I didn't go along: curiosity succumbed to laziness.

I sort of hear voices, Father. I hope this one may interest you, as it does me.

I was reared in the fear of hell; describing the fires, my mother had words at will. And with no words at all she made me ashamed of my body. In the catechism there was more about hell, and a definition of mortal sin, and warnings about the dangers to chastity: idleness, bad companions, improper dances, immodest dress, company-keeping and indecent conversation, books plays and pictures.

When I was eight, I had a summer playmate called Jimmy. His were the first male private parts I ever saw, and one day in a hollow on a hillside, we explored each other, touching, sniffing; I can still hear our silence and the sounds of the sheep and the sea. I understood nothing, but I did feel guilt, and was soon consumed with anxiety about hell. I rehearsed confession, but I couldn't confess; I hid my sin. A sacrilege. And every first Friday, another sacrilege. And Communion every Sunday: worse sacrileges still. When I learned the facts of life, my sin stank all the more.

At twelve I was sent to boarding-school. The nuns vaunted

purity, though vaguely, as a way of being spiritually ladylike. But a retreat master preached with icy precision on the sins of the flesh, and sheep and goats, and hell. I confessed to him afterwards, but I failed to unload my secret.

I never warmed to the nuns. They *boasted* about their vows of poverty, chastity and obedience. But they were less poor than most people I knew. And chastity didn't impress me: I would be saddled with it myself. As for obedience, it stopped none of them from enjoying power. In rebellion, at fifteen, I decided I would serve God better: I would have no power ever, I would be nothing. I took a vow of ignorance: not even the name of a street would I learn if I didn't need to know it. I left school that summer, and stayed at home, helping my father with the sheep, my mother with the children.

My sin stayed with me, like a dull ache mostly, occasionally engulfing me in panic. Until one day I told it to a priest. Pádraig de Brún his name was; he was head of the University in Galway and he had a house in Dun Chaoin. I met him near Kruger's and he walked a bit of the road with me. He had an honest face, and on impulse, I blurted out my story. He stopped up on the road and put his hand on my head, and he said (I'm translating): "Oh, you poor girl! And that has been eating at you for ten years. God help us. Sure what was in it only the curiosity of a child? Don't be afraid of your body, girl; 'twas God gave it to you. I hope you'll learn to feel free, and to enjoy yourself; why don't you start going to the dances? And every day that I live I'll say a prayer for you, that you'll have peace."

Peace is too weak a word to describe what descended on me and remained with me for a time.

Shortly after that, an aunt of mine in the next parish became bedridden, and I began to go twice a week to help out. A neighbouring lad my own age, who was simple, took a shine to me. He followed me everywhere, in silence, but his attentions didn't bother me. His mother was embarrassed, though, and started keeping him home. And then one night she came to tell me her poor Pádraig was being brought next day to Tralee, to the mental hospital. She had found him sleepwalking a few times, calling out my name; two nights ago he had woken up howling and had howled for hours. He was below in the house now, crying out for me; maybe if I came down for a spell he might quieten. I went willingly.

The boy was in his bed, and when he saw me he went silent. A while later he said, "Come in and lie down here beside me," and with a light heart I did. He fell asleep with his head on my breast, and I soon fell asleep myself. In the morning he said to his mother, "I suppose we might as well go so," and he walked to the pony and trap; the men taking him needed no ropes. He gave no trouble, and walked like a lamb into the hospital, and I never heard of him ever coming out.

For the mother I was a saint, but the curate came to our house that evening and ordered me up to the church for confession. I said I had nothing to confess, and I never entered that church again. I didn't go to Mass elsewhere; instead I rose early on Sunday mornings and cycled to Gallarus oratory. I would sit there a while, looking out to sea and being quiet, sheltering under that upturned stone boat. I never tried to pray, I let the stones do that for me. Sometimes I brought my flute with me and played slow airs.

One morning as I approached the oratory I heard noises from inside; looking in the little back window I saw a young blond couple making love. The kisses, the caresses, the limbs entwined in the sunlight: I thought it was all beautiful. I tiptoed away and reappeared as they were leaving; they were Norwegians who had passed the night there, not knowing what the place was. The hour I spent there that morning was a peaceful one.

The following summer, Clive appeared: a very gentle Englishman, a historian, who wanted to learn Irish. I gave him lessons, and in no time we were in love. We didn't say it, though; we were shy with each other, yet we did relax: we walked and chatted and laughed and swam and lay in the sun, but all without once touching. He knows how hurt I am, I thought; it's his maturity. (At 38, he was exactly twice my age.)

"Come away with me, Katie," he said at the end of the summer. And I did, to the cottage he had rented near Kilkee. We had separate rooms, and though there was still reserve, we were freer with each other, and we were happy.

Some nights he would sit on the edge of my bed, chatting, and one night I asked him to lie with me, for closeness. We lay a long time, quiet, with our arms around each other. He slept then, and I stayed awake, in deep contentment. Around dawn I gave him my first kisses, as gentle as snowflakes, and he awoke; in seconds we were a tangle of passion. But when he touched my secret places, I howled as if entering hell: in a hallucination I was back on the hillside with Jimmy, assailed by the shrieking of priests. I broke free and ran from the house. I stumbled along the beach for an age, convulsed by unaccountable sobbing. Then I washed myself in the sea and came out cold and calm.

"Katie, may my right hand wither if I ever knowingly do you harm," Clive said, when I returned to the house.

"Clive, I want us to make love," I said a few nights later. And we did. I was like a nervous canoe on a river; there was a gentle flow at first; then he steered me through rapids, over a waterfall, down into a churning pool and out into a place of cool quiet light. We lay there, in peace, and I learned what 'two in one' meant.

We blossomed. Life was all pleasure, conversation a delight. We exchanged our stories. He talked about the book he was working on, but I never asked for details. He was amused and impressed by my vow; it made me, he said, very special and precious. I looked after the flowers while he read or wrote. Often we broke off, at any hour, to make love. Some days we walked around naked, hardly aware that we were so.

"The most noxious idea in the Bible," Clive said, "is that when Adam and Eve saw they were naked, they felt ashamed."

I hoped he might ask me to marry him, but it didn't seem urgent. When they called me Mrs Markham in the shops, I smiled with pleasure. I was hoping for a child.

A year later, he told me he was a priest. I went berserk; I tore at him, screaming curses. I attacked our bed; I tried to set fire to the sheets, I ripped horsehair from the mattress; with a poker I disfigured the brass knobs of the bedstead. And I left him that very hour. What devastated me was not his deception; it was that those hands, which knew me inside and out had turned bread into the body of God: I was a walking sacrilege.

I buried myself. In Dublin, for nineteen years. I lived in one room in Cabra, and worked in a shoe-shop nearby. I made no friends. In my time off I walked, walked, walked, anywhere and everywhere: a never-ending pilgrimage to nowhere. A sister kept me informed of family events: weddings, my father's death; I didn't travel. Year after year I watched old shoes walking in, old and new shoes walking out, life passing me by. Memories of Clive assailed me; I routed them in seconds.

Suddenly it was 1968, I was 39. My sister Agnes, married in Rheims, was ill after bearing her third child; I went to help.

Looking after the children, I grieved, for the first time, that I would never have any of my own. I found the streets hard to walk, and after sheltering from a shower one day in the Cathedral, I made it my daily refuge. It was my first holy building since Gallarus, and I'd never seen anything like it. With all the pillars it was like a stone forest; or when I looked at the spectacular stained glass I was a bird in a magnificent cage, drifting mysteriously through space. I would sit in the Blessed Sacrament Chapel before the flickering red lamp, and forget there was a city outside; it was the place that felt nearest to home. I didn't pray. A smiling priest approached me once, but I made it clear we had no common language. Coming in I'd look at the Smiling Angel's statue over the door;

going out I'd look for the sculpture projecting farthest from the façade: a cow's head; it said something about a lost home and made me sad.

Agnes's family moved to Grenoble; I went with them. I went to say goodbye to the Cathedral first, to the stained glass and the red lamp and the angel and the cow; then I walked round the outside in the rain. A line from a school poem repeated itself in my head:

> "*A Dhia, bí liom ar mhá an áir, do ghrásta im chroí*"–
> "*O God be with me on the field of battle, your grace in my heart.*"

There was a gust of wind, and a stone the size of my fist hurtled down from the top of the Cathedral and broke in three pieces at my feet.

I disliked Grenoble. I sat inside at a window, looking to the mountains for relief, but the thunderstorms stirred some spiritual phlegm within me. I grew morose and irritable; Agnes asked me if I wanted to go home. I didn't; I didn't know what I wanted. Gazing out the window at the mountains, I turned 40 in private.

Agnes improved. She began to bring me on pilgrimages. There was a quiet white place called La Grande Chartreuse, where Saint Bruno and his followers lay buried. I liked the little gardens and the quiet cells. There was La Salette, where Our Lady had appeared to a young boy and girl. It was high in the mountains; there were snowflakes although it was June. I was struck by the girl's name, Mélanie: when I heard it I heard a lamb bleating. We drove to a place called Ars, where a parish priest had wrestled with the devil and denounced dancing. His shrivelled little body, uncorrupted, lay above an altar; I didn't like him at all. At Annecy we saw the tombs of St Francis de Sales and St Jeanne Marie de Chantal. Agnes spoke of their beautiful friendship, and said Francis was a very gentle saint. She bought me his book, *Introduction to the Devout Life,* and for days kept asking how I found it. In exasperation I opened it and read this, under the heading 'The sanctity of the marriage-bed':

The elephant, not only the largest but the most intelligent of animals, provides us with an excellent example.

It is faithful and tenderly loving to the female of its choice, mating only every third year and then for no more than five days, and so secretly as never to be seen, until, on the sixth day, it appears and goes at once to wash its whole body in the river, unwilling to return to the herd until thus purified.

Such good and modest habits are an example to husband and wife . . .

I laughed, and then found myself shaking with anger. I ripped the book to pieces, wishing I could do the same to the saint. That same evening the kids watched a wild-life documentary, and when I looked in on them I saw a bull elephant pursuing a cow, his huge tool swinging and dancing. I watched in delight till his goal was accomplished, and there was nothing about washing in a river. I sat down and wrote to the TV station, asking for photographs. A fortnight later I received them, two fine big glossy pictures: the chase and the clumsy climax; they're hanging in my bedroom still.

Our last trip was to Valchevrières, an abandoned village at the foot of the Alps; the inhabitants were wiped out by German forces in 1944. We walked down a long deep valley, past Stations of the Cross; the fourteenth was in the little village church. I walked among the dilapidated houses; it was a holier place than any shrine we'd been to. I looked through a window and saw briars and nettles growing through a bed. And it was *our* bed, the one I had slept in with Clive: the same black iron bars, the same fanlight design, the identically placed brass knobs. I cried, and I cried all the way back to Grenoble, and I cried there too for two days. I couldn't explain to Agnes or Dominique. When I calmed, they said I should return to Ireland, and I agreed.

In Paris I went walking. I saw people streaming in and out of a church. I entered, and saw a nun asleep in a glass case. She had been dead since 1876, a guide was explaining; her name was Sister Catherine Labouré and Our Lady had given her the design for the Miraculous Medal. I bought a medal on a length of blue woollen thread, and left; as I walked I said a few times: "O Mary conceived without sin, pray for us who have recourse to thee"; I was praying to have Clive back.

In a huge square I entered a restaurant; I had trouble explaining what I wanted till an elderly woman in a shapeless blue dress and with an Irish accent invited me to join her. Her name was Kate O'Brien, and she was from Limerick, and she was a writer. I didn't tell her my name. She was drinking a bottle of wine with MACON on the label, and she said she drank it because of Godot: the tramps had been in the Macon country. She had seen a production in Madrid in which Lucky had drooled all through his speech; she didn't know how it was done but it was magnificent. She sighed and quoted:

What do you do? I mind the goats, sir . . . What does your brother do? He minds the sheep, sir . . . We have kept our appointment . . . We are not saints, but we have kept our appointment. How many people can boast as much?

"What a wonderful writer," she said, and sighed again.

She asked me what I had seen in Paris, and I told her about the incorrupt nun. She said many nuns she knew were batty, but some were magnificent; friends of hers said she'd have made a wonderful Reverend Mother. But she had lost her faith at the age of nine; all that praying for things had seemed nonsense to her. She had a friend who threatened to call in the priest when she was dying, but she hoped it wouldn't happen.

No one was interested in her writing now, she said; her last novel, *As Music and Splendour,* had been a failure; it had got no reviews. She was now writing her memoirs and working on her last, longest and most difficult novel, *Constancy*; it started with an Irish girl going to study French in Grenoble. She stopped suddenly and said: "What an interesting face you have!"

I thought hers was noble and honest, and I told her I had loved and left a priest and loved him still.

"You're not Kate Kelleher?" she asked.

I said I was.

"Extraordinary!" she said. "I put you and Clive in my last novel. Oh, well disguised, but you're there. Extraordinary I should meet you."

She told me Clive had consulted her before he abandoned the priesthood; later he had written to her while he was living with me, and again after I'd left him; she hadn't heard from him since. She would send me a copy of the letters. It wouldn't really be a breach of confidence; they would help me to think kindly of him. I told her to address them to Kilkee Post Office. I looked in my bag for some little gift to offer her; it couldn't be the Miraculous Medal, so I gave her one of my pieces of Rheims cathedral.

Our cottage near Kilkee was vacant; I rented it, and found a shoeshop to work in. The letters arrived; I have them by heart. I read the second first. Clive had been afraid to tell me his story:

Ah, I was right to be afraid! The distortion, the grotesque, the inferno! The change of beauty and love into some kind of mediaeval, witch-driven fury.

It was, I suppose, an accurate account. The other letter had been written a month before:

I find it profoundly shocking to be loved. Oh, yes, my mother loved me. And there have been many – ah, so many! – whose love for me has been concern for my immortal soul, – accompanied at times, it is true, by real affection. A few women have called me 'kind', 'caring', 'lovely', and to take such tributes to heart has required adjustment. But to be chosen by a woman as unique companion; to be revered as lovable and precious; to be accepted with my weaknesses, forgiven in advance for my failings; to be enabled to draw some great bolt in my soul and to open for the first time the sluice of my feelings; to face another human being in unashamed nakedness, and to lose and find myself in the awesome intimacy of our embraces: to all this I find it hard to become accustomed. For so long it was literally unimaginable, now I find it scarcely endurable. My sense of gratitude is fierce; *the devotion I gave to God, she has it all . . . There is no question of marriage – at least not in the Catholic Church. I haven't sought a dispensation; it would take ages, and anyway the legalities are of no interest to me now.*

I felt raised up and thrown down. He hadn't said these things to me, and I didn't know if it would have made a difference. But I knew now what love I had destroyed. I entered a desert. In the succeeding weeks and months I dried up. The elephants leered at me from the bedroom wall; I didn't have the energy to take them down.

In August 1974 someone said: "Kate O'Brien is dead; she used to spend her summers in Kilkee as a child."

That day I wrote to Clive, care of his publishers: *'I'm living in our old cottage. I love you. Please wish me well.'*

A month later he knocked on my door. Twenty-four years fell away. We embraced, kissed, laughed, cried, talked. He had loved me always, though he had a partner and two children in Sheffield.

"Let's go to bed", he said.

"Why can't we just love?" I asked, "Why do we have to possess? . . . Oh yes, let's go to bed."

He stayed two days and paid another visit six weeks later. In December he left Polly and came to stay. I wrote to her saying that I was sorry for her suffering but that I couldn't be sorry he was with me.

The next three years were the most sensual of my life. "I think that elephant just winked," was a phrase that provoked bouts of sex. "Fancy an introduction to the devout life?" was another.

(Later that became just "Fancy a bit of devout?") We wallowed.

The devout life ended in November 1977, when Polly kissed her two boys and walked in front of a train. Clive returned from the funeral ten years older, eaten by guilt. He neglected his work and sat for long stretches in silence. In bed he lay away from me, curled up. He brooded continually on death.

But he eventually found peace again, in spasms: he developed dementia; there was confusion and agitation, but respite too. By 1982 he no longer knew me: I was his sister, his mother, the nun who had taught him his catechism . . . I was even Judy Garland or Ingrid Bergman, and the elephants winked again, and to bring him ease I was happy to be anyone or no-one.

He deteriorated. He rose ten times a night and I rose with him. He rambled, he drooled as he babbled, he soiled himself. But I would put him in no old folks' home, I would tend him till death did us part. When God divided the sheep from the goats, he would say to the sheep: "I was incontinent and you made me clean."

Mercifully, in June 1984, he had a heart attack; he woke me screaming my name. I called neither priest nor doctor, I put my Miraculous Medal in his fist, saying, "O Mary conceived without sin . . . " and then "Die, Clive, die!" until he did. Then I held him in my arms for an hour and watched him grow young and beautiful as any saint.

His sons attended the funeral: Arthur, eighteen, and Jason, sixteen. I gave them his books. Over the years there's been a gradual reconciliation.

I help out in an old people's home. I grow the best roses in Clare. I swim every day in the sea. I knit. I've reconnected with my family. I've been to Grenoble, and revisited Valchevrières. I cried there, of course, for all broken loves and broken lives. Agnes told me the name of the place means 'the valley of the girls who mind the goats'.

Nice things happen. Jason dragged me to a cineclub last year in York, and I saw my first two films in one day: *Doctor Zhivago* and *The Deerhunter*. Two moments touched me. Outside a lone house on a vast snow-covered plain, wolves are howling; inside, Yuri and Lara are making love. And Robert de Niro, back from Vietnam, tells Meryl Streep her lover has shot himself. "Why don't we go to bed and comfort each other?" he asks, and they do, in a tiny room beside a railway station, deaf to the clatter of trains. That night I dreamed of a little graveyard. In one corner there was a funeral, all droning and rain; in another, in glorious sunshine, Clive and I made love. On a low wall beside us the Smiling Angel of Rheims sat cross-legged, playing a flute. The sweetness stayed with me for days.

Arthur wrote to me last Christmas. He had read 'The Bridal Night' by Frank O'Connor; it was the most beautiful short story in the world. Could I find him a copy of the book it first appeared in? I did, in a bookshop in Limerick, and next to it was *As Music and Splendour* by Kate O'Brien; I bought that too. It was inscribed: *'To Kate: love always, all ways; Kate.'* I'll never know who Kate was, and, not being a reader, I'll never learn what happened to me either.

I have another book too, a present from my mother for my 65th birthday. It's a lovely-looking book, with a cover like sackcloth. *Miserere* it's called; it's poems by Pádraig de Brún – discovered after his death, my mother told me – with illustrations by some famous French artist. I've never opened it, but I'm grateful for it; now and again I spend a long time reading the title.

That, I imagine, should be your kind of territory, Father Ball. I've been in and out of it myself. I have sympathy for Kate. But she's not innocent; she has made victims . . .

What most clearly reflects my experience in her account is that little prayer she repeats, for very unorthodox purposes: 'O Mary conceived without sin, pray for us who have recourse to thee.' That comes out of my adolescence, for aspirations – 'ejaculations' was their other name – were a practice enjoined by my religious educators, and that was one of their favourites. Saints, they told us, fired off telephone numbers of them; Father Willie Doyle, a Jesuit priest, reached the prodigious total of over a hundred thousand a day. I built up my own little collection – a dozen or so – and used them for a variety of purposes, but especially to repel assaults on my purity. When I lost my faith at 19 they became a nuisance; when I lost my virginity at 21 they embarrassed me. I mounted a campaign to oust them with something more congenial: I repeated lines of poetry or prose and titles of books: 'Our revels now are ended', 'For we are most artistically caged', 'I'm puttin' on me moleskin trousers', 'No-one is anything', 'We won't always be miserable, we'll die yet', 'Les gens sont cons', 'I never promised you a rose-garden', 'By Grand Central Station I sat down and wept' . . .

Some years later, in depression, I wanted to believe again, and tried to invest these compulsive darts with a spiritual import; some contortion was called for, and the effort didn't last long; neither did my crisis of unbelief. And as the years passed and my view of women grew less refined, literature gave way mostly to sex: 'Get moving or get mounted', 'Cut the crap and show us your willy', 'I rode her mother at Fairyhouse', 'Shleamhnaigh sé isteach i ngan fhios dom', 'Only two things smell like fish, and one of them's fish', 'J'ai fait l'amour sans amour' . . . . All this was fine until, during one of my 'episodes', I began repeating these things out loud; the first one I shouted at a female Garda, the second at her male colleague. When I emerged from hospital, I had a new aspiration: 'Cool head, shut mouth'. I have been heard to mutter that too, but it's been out of habit, not illness.

I suppose you've noticed how Kate is hurt by churchy things, yet finds some solace in more of the same. She may not be, at the end, a pratiquante, *or much of a* croyante, *but the Hound of Heaven is doubtless biding his time: I'll wager, as someone said of someone else, that she'll die with the host in her mouth. Am I foretelling my own fate? The Force forbid.*

I confess to a certain curiosity about the incorrupt corpses of saints, but Kate took me by surprise when she said her lover became as beautiful as any saint. Saints beautiful? If I saw some I could judge. It galls me to see my kids' moral education entrusted to the likes of you. (Though it would gall me too to have it left to the likes of me.)

Yours half resentfully,

Enda Ring.

P.S. I had an e-mail today from the man who destroyed my faith. "The important thing," *he writes,* "is to be honest. And being honest, paying attention to what my senses and my reason tell me, I have to say that I regard all believers, especially the more committed ones, as dishonest or psychologically aberrant." *Can you suggest a response, Father? Something from Sheahan's* Apologetics, *perhaps, which taught us, as one of my classmates put it, 'to prove the existence of God from a bike'?*

MOTHER

Dear Helen Archer,

Of all my acquaintances you are one of the most real. Rue St Isidore, Brussels, where you grew up, has had as much impact on me as odd corners of Paris, Seville, Venice . . . And Sainte-Fontaine, the austere novitiate at Bruges, I have done time with you there, under leaden Flemish skies. I know the school you directed in this country as well as I know my own: its tree-lined walks, its lake, its encircling hills. And you yourself have walked ahead of me since I first met you, an example – though not for emulation – of risks survived and virtues won.

You – or was it your Mother General? – got me sacked from my first job. (Well, actually, I was permitted to resign.) I was teaching in a convent school in the midlands, and had to take religious knowledge as well as French and English. To get the students to reflect on the difficulty of moral judgements, I drew on an incident from your life. I explained how, on discovering your father's homosexuality, you had flung yourself into a life of negation and bitterness, but had become gradually humanised, to the point where, at 29, you refused to condemn some sexual misdemeanour by another nun, thus eliciting from your Mother

General the remark: 'So young? Yet already you don't know right from wrong?' Not 'yet', I stressed, in case they hadn't taken it in, not 'still', but 'already'. They liked it.

I was shortly afterwards propositioned by the mother of one of my pupils, a most attractive young 40 year old. To encourage me, she told me that if I refused, she would have me dismissed for teaching heresy. I did, and she had.

I was in such shock for ages that I couldn't apply for another job. I didn't even move out of the area. Eventually, on my uppers, I approached the lady for help; I ended up, as I suspected I might, in her bed. There followed a six-month affair during which I was . . . well, kept. Eventually, weary of subterfuge and urged on by a reawakening self-respect, I upped and left.

I can't say I kept you much in view during that half-year, but I have since then often brought you sharply into focus, when I have needed to watch you endure. Because, whatever about the evolution or subtleties of your thought, that is what you most persistently did: you endured, – among other things, an unrelenting confinement. Which is precisely how I characterise my own existence.

I should be grateful if, as someone concerned for hurt children, you could take the time to peruse the attached pages. You might first like to consider this thought from Dame Julian of Norwich, from whom I heard last week; I have no use for it: 'God rejoices that he is our father, and God rejoices that he is our mother, and God rejoices that he is our very husband, and our soul his beloved wife.'

I got the kick of a horse. On the back of the head and the side of the head. That's why I'm simple. That's what they call me. I forget things. I remember some things. Some things are fuzzy. More are like a puzzle. I can't read any more. I can't write.

Daddy had a better stallion than anyone else. A big black one.

Mares used to come from everywhere. To be covered. That's what they called it. Covered. I didn't like watching. I'd go off with the dog. Angel I called him. A collie. Always running around, yelping. And sniffing at everything. We went everywhere. He slept on the end of my bed.

I loved milking. I'd have my head in again' the cow, getting the smell of her. I used to put my hand up inside her leg, to get the ticks. Big fat grey fellows full of blood, with young black ones on their heads. I loved cows calving. One of our cows had twin calves. Bull calves. I called them Tony and Joe, like the twins the Sergeant's missus was after having. Daddy hit me a belt in the mouth. He didn't like the Sergeant. I don't know why. He didn't like other people liking him.

One night I was in bed and I heard him shouting at Mammy: "Throw away them crutches, you bitch! Only letting on to be a cripple! For fear I'd throw the leg over you! You'd no fear of the Sergeant, you whore you!"

No one was afeard of the Sergeant. Everyone liked him. Mammy said one time that Daddy was a proud man.

I couldn't stand cats. We had an orangey one and she had six kittens and she took the heads off every one of them.

I liked pigs when they were bonavs. When they were big they just lay in their shite. Pigs' shite had a rotten smell. Every shite had a different smell. Horse-shite, cowshite, pigshite, people-shite. I didn't like the smell of petrol or exhaust. There were grand smells on the bog. And making hay.

There was always work. Sowing spuds and picking spuds. Thinning beet, pulping mangolds, feeding calves. I was no good to work, Daddy said. That's why he wouldn't buy me a bike. In the holidays he used to call me real early. He'd pull me out of the bed and shout: "Sleep, sleep! That's all you want, sleep! You'll never do anything worthwhile in your sleep! Get up, you pup!"

He used to beat me sometimes, even before I got dressed. It was worse than school. I didn't like school that much. Sums and reading and all that. I was bright enough, but I wouldn't settle. That's what the teacher told Mammy. The teacher was nice. She told us your first Communion is like your first kiss from God.

I loved football. And conkers. Some fellows used to blow up frogs. Stick a straw up their arse. It used to make me sick.

I used to serve Mass. The lads were all afraid of Father Morley. I had a jigsaw one time and we were making it in the vestry, on the table beside the Massclothes. Father Morley came in early and one of the boys swept the jigsaw onto the floor. I was picking up the pieces while he was putting on his Massclothes. He asked me what I was doing under his feet, and I said looking for my jigsaw Father and he only laughed.

It was my job to ring the Angelus. I loved that. One time I pulled too hard on the rope and the bell got stuck upside down in the concrete. When they got it down there were dints in the concrete. They're still there. There was no more Angelus then. Daddy only laughed. He said 'twas too much fucking Angelus we had.

I used to love the Stations of the Cross in the chapel. The priest going around to the pictures, and the candles and the colours and the people genuflecting: '*We adore thee O Christ and we praise thee because by thy Holy Cross thou hast redeemed the world.*'

I loved that prayer. I know the Our Father and the Hail Mary and the Glory Be and that prayer. *We adore thee O Christ and we praise thee.* That's my favourite.

I loved all about the Holy Spirit too. When the teacher told us about the Holy Spirit I used to look around quick over my shoulder to see if I could see him slipping in unknown to us through the window. Tongues of fire. I loved that. I used to watch leaves falling and think they were tongues of fire. Licking the ground. *And thou shalt renew the face of the earth.* And the ground would start talking strange talk.

Looking for birds' nests was my favourite. I found 32 one summer. There could be sixteen eggs in a wren's nest, all moss, the size of a sliothar with a hole in the side. Pigeons' nests were simple, you could make them yourself. Swallows only make half nests, up again' a wall. Hedgesparrows' eggs are as blue as blue. They're the loveliest things, they're my all time favourite. Cuckoos can lay different kinds of eggs. Some of them are blotchy. I never saw one, I was told. I rathered eggs than the little birds that come out of them.

Mammy died. I was eleven or ten. She fell into the river. Daddy had an argument with the Sergeant after the funeral. He beat me that night. He used to often beat me after that. I ran away with Angel after I got my Confirmation.

They sent me away to live in a school. They took Angel off me. There were fellows from everywhere. I was no good at most things. I loved woodwork. And cooking, and gardening. I liked handball too. I learned to play the mouth organ. 'The Boys of Blue Hill' and 'Scotland the Brave'. I sang on the stage at a concert. 'The Mountains of Pomeroy' and 'Poor Old Joe'.

I missed Angel, and the cows and the smells. I had fits twice near the tuck shop when I saw fellows sucking lollipops. I wasn't allowed near the tuck shop any more.

I watched everybody. I knew something about everybody. They didn't always tell me themselves, other fellows who knew them told me sometimes. There were quare fellows there. Willie Creed was retarded. He could tell you in three seconds the day of the week you were born. Even what day it was the day your father was born. Jerry Burke had six fingers on each hand. Paddy Mooney was as bald as an egg and he only fifteen. Jack Egan had half a purple face. He was my friend. When we were washing ourselves I never used to look at myself in the mirror. I hated mirrors I was that ugly. I don't care now. I used to wet the bed sometimes.

Some of the priests gave sermons about hell. I didn't give a damn, I knew I wasn't going there. There was a choir for the church, in Latin. I loved that. *Credo in unum Deum, something omnipotentem.* There was another class of a song too, I'll sing it for you:

Gaudens gaudebo in Domino, et exultabit anima mea in Deo meo: quia induit me vestimentis salutis: et indumento justitiae circumdedit me, quasi sponsam ornatam monilibus suis.

I do sing them words often, they're mighty, I rather them than Abba. I know what it means too, 'cause Father Frawley would flatten your ear for you if you didn't learn the Latin. It means:

I will greatly rejoice in the Lord, and my soul shall be joyful in my God: for he hath clothed me with the garments of salvation, and with the robe of justice He hath covered me, as a bride adorned with her jewels.

I finished in the school. The Sergeant collected me. He told me Daddy didn't want me. I didn't want him either. The Sergeant had a cottage down a lane, half a mile from our house. It was empty, and he said I could live in it. For rent I could mow the lawn. He gave me a bike. Angel was dead a good while.

My first day back I went to the forge. That's where I got the kick of a horse. I was knocked out for a good few weeks. I was in the hospital. Then I came to the cottage. The Sergeant brings me food. I cook it myself.

The Sergeant called me in the middle of the night. He was banging on the door for ages in the mist before I woke up. He told me our house was after going on fire and Daddy was after being burnt alive in his bed. I didn't cry. I think I was too sleepy. The Sergeant put his hand on my head and my shoulder.

"You're all wet," he said. "You must be sweating." He gave a few sniffs at me and he looked at the wheels of my bike. Someone must have brought it round from the back of the house.

The day after the funeral I went to go and mow the lawn. There was no petrol in the can. I thought there would be some. I was bothered. I asked the Sergeant did he ever hear of anyone being able to ride a bike in his sleep. Or start a fire. Could that happen?

"Ah no, son," he said. "No, no, that could never happen, not at all, no, no, no."

There's a thing, he told me, that's called an act of God. I was happy after that.

After I got the kick of the horse, I started to remember some things. Daddy used to give me lollipops. After making me do things to him. 'Afters' he called the lollipops. And he used to put me on his bed and cover me. The way a stallion covers a mare. The first time was the day of my first Communion. If Daddy was alive, and if I told the Sergeant, Daddy'd be dead.

I hope you haven't been offended by the grosser items in the above account. There is no autobiography here to speak of. Details were, of course, supplied by childhood memories – of relations with my parents, Mass-serving, summers in the country, boarding-school . . . but there are important transpositions. For example, one of my jobs was to light a fire in my father's study on all but the hottest evenings. I came to resent the task, as it interrupted my amusements. I indulged my resentment on one occasion by sitting in front of the fire and fantasizing about burning down the house. I nodded off and evidently keeled over, for the next thing I knew, I was screaming with pain, and my father's jacket was quenching the flames in my hair. I was excused fire duty after that, but for some reason I became obsessed with the notion that my father would die in a fire. He didn't, as it happens, he should have been so lucky. Another influence on the story, in all likelihood, was a lecture I heard recently on the role of the bicycle in the works of Beckett, Flann O'Brien and John McGahern. (It wasn't up to much.) Thank you for your attention, Mother Helen; I know you have onerous duties.

Yours sincerely,

Enda Ring.

MAN

14 September

Dear . . . Man,

I've read bits and pieces about the Shroud that housed you: scourge wounds, nail marks, linen patterns, pollen, blood, fifteenth century, first century, carbon dating, miracle, fake . . . And I can't get worked up over whether you are Leonardo da Vinci or Jesus.

I first saw the Shroud donkey's years ago, when I wandered into the church in Turin where it's kept; I had never heard of it before. I was stupefied, but it did not revive my faith. Two impressions remain, however. First, I regard the positive of which the Shroud bears the negative as the noblest image of a human face and body on this earth. Second, that face is the only one I know which summons the viewer to absolute sincerity: if I were a believer I'd say it offers a preview of the particular judgement.

It was no doubt my regard for the Shroud which prompted me, during my earliest 'episode', to wear a slit sheet as a poncho, and to parade, otherwise naked, through the streets of Galway, proclaiming to the people that there was no God, that they were the only gods.

You know St Augustine's witticism: Inter urinam et faeces nascimur: Between piss and shit we are born? *It would make a good epigraph for this story I invite you to read. The story itself I would call* The Crack.

Like the Islandman, I was at my mother's breast till I was four. "I want a drink from your little mountains," I used to tell her. She was always happy to oblige; she enjoyed it, she told me later, and she knew she could have no more children. ("I nearly didn't have you," she added.)

We were both mad about my father. He used to dance around the kitchen, with me on his shoulders laughing; I never felt safer anywhere though everything was moving under me. He told me stories, and I always asked for more.

"Life is a story God is telling us," he would say sometimes; "let that keep you going till the next time."

My mother taught me to read before I went to school, and she kept me supplied with books. Sometimes she'd interrupt my reading with a hug and say: "You're my favourite youngster, Pat; yourself and the Child of Prague."

I was a happy child. I think I thought every child was.

My father died when I was twelve; he was painting the ceiling of the North Chapel and he fell onto the altar. He was buried beside a row of cypresses. I stopped believing in God; my mother didn't argue.

I buried myself in study, and during holidays I devoured books. My mother's boss gave her a couple of hundred novels when I was fifteen. She kept one big one from me. I burrowed into the rest.

After my Leaving Cert I planned a summer job, a holiday, then enrolment in UCC, across the river. The job was with a plumber; what I did – most often on my own – was to free blocked sewer-pipes. In August I went hostelling.

I met Olive in Doolin. She came from seven miles outside Cork and was a music student. We were drawn to each other and decided to travel together. On the quayside at Kinvara two nights later, we sheltered from a shower under a boat. "It's like a little church in here," Olive said, and the next thing we were kissing – surprised, both of us, and tentative and shy. Next afternoon we followed a river walk near Spiddal, and halted where a waterfall gushed through a crack in a massive rock. We sat in silence for a while, the torrent between us. Then we came together and lay and kissed, and removed each other's clothing. When my lips discovered her breasts I thought: Perfection exists . . . Afterwards we swam naked in the pool below.

That week, travelling, was idyllic. And the next one, when we stayed in Olive's house; her parents were on holiday, and her twin brothers – fishermen – were at sea. We walked, talked, laughed, listened to music, and made love, and made love, and made love. It was a few days, but it was a kind of eternity; we were outside time. And on the Friday night the twins arrived unexpectedly and found us embracing in the bath, to the strains of Mahler's Resurrection Symphony. They punched and kicked us, then shoved me down the stairs. The last I saw of Olive, she was lying on the landing, blood pumping from her nose.

"I love you, Pat, I love you, I'll see you," she called after me.

They threw me into their van and drove to some lonely place; all I could see when we stopped were stone crosses in a graveyard. They dragged me to a dried-up well, tied my feet with a blue rope, and lashed the other end to a tree; then they lowered me head first, and emptied a box of fish in after me. I spent two nights and a day there, fainting and waking. I was rescued by some travellers who saw the rope; they brought me to hospital, and I recovered in a couple of days. I pretended I didn't know my assailants, and I told my mother nothing.

I didn't dare try to contact Olive; I waited for her to get in touch with me. She didn't. It was my second bereavement. But soon there was a distraction: my mother had a stroke the week before College opened. She was left partly paralysed, and virtually without speech. I decided to forego my studies and look after her myself. For part-time work, I opted to unblock sewer-pipes. I bought my own bike, rods, overalls and wellies. I depended on word of mouth and a printed card; I went from one or two calls a week to three a day. By the time I'd have had a BA, I was known throughout the city as Pat the Pipes.

I read. Two or three novels a week. And every so often I encountered perfection: *The Portrait of a Lady, The Go-Between, The Land of Spices* . . . It was hard to go out to work then, or cook a meal; I wanted to savour my melancholy elation, my static, mute compassion for us all.

I read to my mother: *Pride and Prejudice, David Copperfield, Le Père Goriot, Anna Karenina, Thérèse Desqueyroux, Mister Johnson, At Swim-Two-Birds, The Chosen* . . . With her couple of dozen words she managed comments: "Clown! . . .", "Craythur . . .", "Hussies! . . .", "Blackguard! . . .", "Go on . . ." When I finished *The Leopard*, my own favourite, she just said "Ah . . .", and went into an hour-long silence.

My mother, my books, my sewers: that was my life. There was an emptiness. I ached to possess some perfection. Or to create it . . . The idea came to me of writing my own novel . . . For months I struggled with questions: What about? How? Why? And I saw, if I were to do anything, that it was imperative, and impossible, to do something *new*. I floundered. And then, on my twenty-third birthday, a journalist said to me: "Life is a newspaper, not a novel", and I saw it: a novel in the form of a newspaper. It would not be strong on story; but it could picture a community's life, make palpable the million links that bind its members, sketch in snatches of background, and prompt guesses as to what's to come. The items could be read in an infinity of sequences; each one could illuminate others, and contribute to the epiphany of the whole; a classified ad. overlooked could rob the total picture of some lustre.

I told my mother; she banged the arm of her wheelchair and said: "Do!" I got to work.

I invented a city. The map took weeks, then hung on the kitchen wall. Key inhabitants were conceived on index-cards. Snippets were entered provisionally in a dummy newspaper. I attended reluctantly to the sewers. In streets and houses I observed as never before; I co-opted characters, imagined behaviours. Instead of novels, I perused the occasional newspaper.

I became appalled by what I'd started. It was the jigsaw of ten thousand pieces, the impossible game of patience. After nine months, I considered quitting. I told my mother; she said: "Stick!" I stuck at it. I took a few decisions, and I was writing.

Six more years hard labour lay ahead, with breaks for discouragement and self-doubt. Was it a colossal waste of time? Would I ever finish? Would it matter if I didn't? Would it benefit anybody? Without my mother I would not have persevered. She followed every detail. I bounced ideas off her: I might say, for example: "Four priests have been murdered. The killer is the bishop; the clue is in the crossword. And he's having an affair with the Superintendent; you can work that out from the chess problem." And she would laugh and bang her arm-rest and say: "Lovely!"

I had no scruples about inventing an impossible story; there is no such thing: anything that can happen, can happen. The bones of my novel were those of the typical Irish weekly: political controversy, industrial disputes, corruption, drugs, murder, rape, incest, sport and so on. The flesh was in the women's page, agony aunt, editorials, kiddies' corner, film reviews, ads, obituaries, letters to the editor, thought for the week and *cúpla focal* column. Final touches came from coverage of meetings, launches, appointments, retirements, concerts, prize-givings, weddings, fires and funerals.

For photographs I had three solutions: out of focus, rear view and no heads. The only exception concerned my mother: as the work neared completion she asked to be included, as a joke, among the Anniversary notices and their nauseating doggerel. Beneath a twenty-year old photograph I wrote:

Oh Mother you were an absolute dote;
When I think of you I get a lump in my throat;
You're finished with wheelchairs now and everything like that;
If there was a heaven I'm sure you'd be in it, your ever-loving
Pat.

113

This related to nothing else in the paper, but I was happy to give my mother special treatment. I had already made a couple of Hitchcock-type appearances myself. One was in an ad. under 'Services Available' which was linked to two other items: a feature on the current boom in drugs, and a report on a recent Dutch tour by the local pipe band. The suggestion in my ad was that the gear had been smuggled into Ireland in the musicians' instruments: 'Serious shit? Pat the Pipes, 307105'. My other appearance was under my (little-known) real name, Pat Piper: I featured in a book review as the author of an imaginary novel about the traditional music scene, called *The Crack*. The review's thrust – 'Piper exposes the earth beneath the mirth' – mirrored the newspaper's motto (my novel's Joycean epigraph): *erde from merde.*

I toyed with various titles: *The Gutter Press, The Stink, The Novel Idea, The True Lie* . . . I settled eventually on *The Crack.*

On my thirtieth birthday, 4 April 1992, *The Crack* went on sale. At 6 a.m. I collected five thousand copies from the printers. I brought them home – I had a van at this stage – and put most of them in the spare room; they were dated simply 'Saturday' and I would sell them later in other cities. My mother was thrilled. "Pleased," she said, "well pleased," and kissed me.

By 8.00 I was selling to the public. At the junction of Patrick Street and Cook Street I took my stand, beside the Echo Boy, a new lifesize bronze statue of a newsboy. I identified with his enthusiasm and I gave substance to his silent cries.

I was successful beyond my dreams. It seemed everyone was intrigued and wanted to buy. I could have believed that all my plumbing customers had come out to cheer me on. Twice during the morning I had to renew my supplies, and bank cash. I grew graceful in my movements, radiant in my smiling, eloquent in my patter.

I forgot to have lunch. In the afternoon bustle I continued to do well. Several people came back to ask abut the truth of my fiction, and I delivered impromptu lectures on the spot. Some of my listeners bought extra copies. I grew elated.

I had a snack at tea-time and then moved to Grand Parade. Outside the cinema my sales continued. I was bubbling with happiness, and it seemed to be infectious. By dark, my euphoria was extreme. I walked the streets and handed *The Crack* out free. I was thinking: 'I have come into my own! This city is my own, these are my people, my friends.' I stuffed copies through the letterboxes of all the business premises on the South Mall; at traffic lights I pushed copies through car windows, telling people to enjoy *The Crack*. At one in the morning a crowd of set-dancers emerged from a hotel; I bestowed a copy on everyone I could reach. Everyone, everything, was beautiful; my city was familiar and transfigured. At a burger joint a man shouted in to a woman, "Enjoy your supper, bitch!" and it sounded like an invitation to a banquet. Couples strolling, or chatting under street-lights, were embodiments of perfect love and bliss; I tiptoed up and on them too conferred my favours. I was gathering my friends in for a supper.

A young man overtook me. I pursued him, pressed a copy of my novel on him. "Fuck off!" he hissed, and I'd never seen such hatred in a face. I retraced my steps, and spotted a copy of *The Crack* in a waste bin. Further on I saw two more, trampled with curry-boxes and squashed chips. There were few people around now, and I began to feel cold; I headed for my van in Perry Street.

I passed close to the Echo Boy; his mouth was full of cigarette-ends and ashes. I felt depressed. A little later I saw the man who had shouted near the burger joint; a young woman was lying at his feet, bleeding from the mouth and crying: "But I love you, Pat, I love you, I love you!" She was the image of Olive: the same shock of short yellow hair, the same fine, delicate, strong features. I felt horror and panic. I hurried on, teeth chattering, muttering a misquotation: "Even the Olives lie bleeding . . ., even the Olives lie, bleeding . . ." I was in a cold sweat, I thought I tasted blood on my lips.

When I got home, the front door was unlocked, and I found my mother dead. Murdered. A crucifix had been rammed down her throat – the one that had hung over her bed. I remember shrieking "Daddy! Daddy!" before I fainted.

In the days that followed I raged, coldly. I had no tears; I wanted blood. I looked icily into each sympathising eye. Beneath the cypresses, I hardly saw the coffin going down; I was scanning the heads among the headstones, seeking out the eye of the killer I wished to kill.

I stripped the house bare. The mirrors came down, and the calendar and the clock, and the holy-water font and the Sacred Heart and The Child of Prague with his glued-on head. I folded away the tapestry that depicted the Last Supper, and dumped the sofa whose ugliness it failed to redeem. I sold all but a dozen of my books. Of the spare room I made a little desert. I burned all copies of *The Crack*; for days black ashes polluted Sunday's Well.

Emptying my mother's room I found the novel she kept from me years ago; it dealt with the Spanish Civil War and was called *The Cypresses Believe in God*.

They never found her killer.

I still unblock sewers. I still read, but not novels. I sit in the spare room most days, trying to find whether there's something at the heart of nothing.

On weekends I climb mountains. I've yet to find one that hides all traces of humanity. Where I can forget Christ's feet protruding from my mother's mouth. A mist rolled in from the Blaskets one day when I was on top of Mount Eagle; I spent eighteen hours there, seeing neither outside nor inside. It was the nearest I've come to relief from the desolation that consumes me always, whether I'm driving my van, or reading *King Lear*, or checking my breasts for lumps, or shoving shit into Cork Harbour.

This story owes little to novels or sewers: its genesis is an incident I've tried to forget . . . Back in 1982, I spent some months surveying the placenames mentioned on tombstones in the county's graveyards. One blustery Tuesday morning in May, I arrived at my last cemetery, in Poul, miles from anywhere. I had ten minutes work done when I noticed a blue rope stretched tautly from the top of the tallest Celtic cross in the place. I went to investigate, and found, in a deep hollow beside the cross, the body of a teenage girl, heavily pregnant. A silver cross and chain were tangled in the noose. The body was still warm, but she was definitely dead. I was on my way to the car to raise the alarm when it occurred to me that I didn't want the place cordoned off for days, with gardaí snooping around and pathologists coming and going. There was an important publication riding on my survey, and there was a deadline, and the alarm could wait. I continued my work for two days, becoming genuinely oblivious to the corpse. In the evenings I didn't socialize or heed the media, so I heard nothing about anyone missing. I returned the third morning to decipher some older tombstones, and was met by a pack of dogs, among them one horrible black brute with a silver cross hanging from his mouth. I fled, and ten miles away called the gardaí anonymously from a public phone. Did I attend the funeral? You know I didn't: apart from anything else what was left of her was buried in Poul. It transpired that she was the daughter of the girl who had given me my first kiss; her unborn child was also a girl.

I never completed my survey, and haven't published a word since. Beside some deeds, mere murders pale.

What should be done to the likes of me? What should I do to myself? Could I, like something in Dante, be buried in piss and shit, and be reborn?

Yours abjectly,

Enda Ring.
P.S. Here ends my penning. For six weeks now, in a game of 'Trick or Truth?', I've tossed off epistles and yarns. In pairs. Admiring my mirrors . . . I'm all done with mirrors. I've seen the light – cold light – in the glace of my own dark soul.

Exit, pursued by a bier.

PLAYER

Dear William Shakespeare,

I regard you as more than human, our closest approach to a divine incarnation . . . Your work mocks all other works, exposes their pitiful futility. If they'd sense, even the big fellows would pack up and go home: Blake, Tolstoy, Joyce, pebbles at the butt of Everest.

Does everyone have a story of your effect on them, or, for most, are you locked in books? A friend told me that seeing Othello had unleashed in him fearful jealousy concerning his wife. I can cap that. The first time I made love with a woman, she fell asleep before me, and I lay a long time looking on her loveliness. I tired eventually and reached to switch off the lamp. My mind was suddenly invaded by a line Othello speaks before smothering Desdemona: 'Put out the light, and then put out the light'; it said itself over and over as I turned back to see again the glow on her cheek and neck. Sexual desire flared in me, and a mad urge to end her life. I switched off the lamp. Othello's words and my heartbeat were sounding and pounding together. I placed my hands on her shoulders and worked my way up to her neck; I was sweating from every pore . . . I began to exert pressure, and

121

she awoke; I shot back into sanity. She went to the bathroom and I grabbed my clothes and bolted; I pulled on my jeans on the stairs, slipped into my shoes on the street. I never again visited a prostitute. I was left with the knowledge that I was really capable of killing. (Oddly enough, I had a note some days ago from the Prince of Salina; it said simply: 'Come down out of your head. Get thee to a whorehouse. I wish you joy of your own Marianinna.')

I take the liberty of sending you a story. I'm not asking that you read it; what matters is that I get rid of it; that is therapy. (And to who else should I send this?)

Oh yes, there's another thing. Years ago a girlfriend wrote me off as emotionally autistic, and left me with this couplet, inscribed on the back of a photo of myself that she returned:

> *An island heart, cut off from flesh and blood,*
> *Whose dreams of love shall founder in the flood.*

That's not yours, is it? I mean, you did write a fair bit of mediocre stuff . . . I expect you can't remember. Well, anyway, I found it very hurtful. But she predicted right.

The story I'm part of is very well known, yet nobody knows about me.

My childhood was not happy. My father regretted my birth and ignored me. My brother called me Adopta, my sister called me Aborta. They treated my mother no better. She was kind to me. She didn't smile much, but she was serene. And strong. Once when I cried – I was eight – she said: "You will be a strong woman," and whenever I cried after that she made me repeat through my tears: "I will be a strong woman."

She was forever singing:

> *For you and I have a guardian angel . . .* , and
> *Ah, sweet mystery of life, at last I've found thee . . .*

She never got beyond those lines, and from hearing them thousands of times I took them for truths; we both had guardian angels and she had found the mystery of life. I never asked her what it was, I assumed I had to find it myself.

And then she died. I was twelve. I didn't cry. Laid out in her coffin, she told me that I had a guardian angel, that she had *really* found the mystery of life, and that I would be a strong woman.

I took everything in: tears, handshakes, hearse, undertakers, wreaths, priests, cards, Mass, singing, prayers: *Do not hold her sins against her, Lord, for in her heart she always desired to do Your will.*

I was observing an elaborate spectacle; I recorded every face, every action. The coffin was bumped down into place, the hole cloaked with a green cover; the crowd dispersed. I stayed to watch the gravediggers filling in, to hear the clay thumping. And suddenly I saw myself in the spectacle. I observed myself observing, and I was more interesting than anybody.

I moved in to live with the Lethams. Yes, *the* Lethams, Olaf and Trudi. Being Dad's employers, they couldn't do enough for us, and when I asked they said yes; Dad didn't object. It just meant moving from the sixth floor to the seventh. I saw young Olaf a lot then. He was fifteen, and he spoke often about becoming an actor. The parents laughed it off: what about the empire he was to inherit? He was very sexy at moments like that.

I was fourteen when Olaf senior made a pass at me. I wasn't angry, just fascinated. I thought: 'I'll say yes to the likes of this when I feel like it'. And I slapped him across the face. When I saw him shrink I knew I had power.

Olivia – my sister – was going out with young Olaf at this stage. At sixteen, she was a year younger than he. Dad warned her against him. And Laurence – my brother – who used to be Olaf's friend, called Olivia Humpty-Dumpty: "First he'll hump you, then he'll dump you. And all the king's horses and all the king's men won't be able to put you together again."

He taunted her with a line from a song: *Keep your legs together coming home from the wake.*

She didn't tell me all this; Olaf did.

Olaf went to Cornell to study business, though he still spoke of a career in theatre. During holidays he was all over Olivia. Towards the end of his second year his father's Rover went over a cliff. Suicide, accident – even murder: nothing could be ruled in or out. His brother Claude took charge of the empire. Olaf stayed home for months, in a black torpor. Even Olivia couldn't help.

The following Easter Claude and Trudi married quietly in Rome. I was pleased. The apartment needed a man, and Claude was a fine specimen. Olaf was shattered. He neglected himself, slept in his car, moped. Trudi's charms were powerless. Olivia dumped him.

Eventually his energy returned. He burst into my room one morning, singing:

> *From a jack to a king,*
> *From loneliness to a wedding ring;*
> *I played an ace and I won a queen;*
> *You made me king of your heart.*

And then he hissed, "That fucker killed my father!"

I forget what I said, and he continued, "Don't you see? This is *Hamlet!* We're up to our necks in it!"

I didn't know the play, and he kept nagging at me to read it. I wouldn't: *Julius Caesar* in school was enough for me.

He accused Dad of lusting after his own daughter. He did an Elvis impersonation and stalked Olivia, in silence. He ambushed Claude repeatedly in the same garb, sang "Uh-huh-huh," at him, and sashayed off. To me he said,

"To be or not to be is not the only question. I'll swing for that motherfucker yet!"

I had to laugh: with his dander up he was the spit of his uncle, except for the Yankee way he pronounced that nasty word.

He had a vicious go at Olivia and left her hysterical: he told her she belonged in a whorehouse run by my father. He was shaking after that. He packed a bag straight away and left.

"I have to get out of this," he said, "or I'll go mad."

Three postcards arrived together from London, three portraits: Charles the First for Trudi, Oliver Cromwell for Claude and Charles the Second for me. I didn't know what was going on.

Three weeks later he walked in and joined us for lunch. Yes, London was lovely. He'd been working in the theatre. No, not acting: on the technical side. A play by Agatha Christie: *The Mousetrap*. He was calmer than I'd ever seen him. I was sunbathing on the roof later and he joined me. What work had he been doing with *The Mousetrap*? He was in charge of the cheese, he told me, and he bit me on the inside of the thigh. He went off laughing.

That night I heard him stamping around the apartment, calling, "Mother!"

He pushed in the door of the guest bedroom and found Claude pinning me against the wardrobe. He put a knife to Claude's throat. Claude backed out the door.

"You came very close," Olaf told him.

He turned to me then, touched my cheek, and asked if I was all right. He was trembling. I laid my hands on his shoulders and said, "Relax."

Minutes later we were between the sheets. Just before he came he cried out: "You're my first!" and I knew it was true.

Then he whispered my name into my neck and hair and ear.

Half an hour later he killed my father. No knife; he didn't lay a finger on him. Found him in Trudi's room, discussing business. Advanced on him, staring. One word: "Daughter-fucker!"

Dad backed away, onto the balcony, over.

Laurence was touring in France and couldn't be located; Olivia was too distraught to attend the funeral; that made me the chief mourner. I didn't mourn much. I had the most curious sensation. I lived every instant intensely. And I was back at my mother's funeral. I was in two times at the one place. Everything was double, nostalgic and fresh. And extraordinarily fascinating.

The police had questions, of course. But Trudi and Olaf satisfied them. Then he got ready to go away. "I have to get out of this play," he said, "or I'll destroy the lot of us. Read *Hamlet*, will you!"

"Life is interesting enough," I answered.

He spent that night with me.

Olivia went from bad to worse. She cut up a pair of Dad's trousers and passed the pieces round as relics in the street. She stripped off beside his grave and walked home dressed in his wreaths. She sat in her room and drank her own urine from a Budweiser bottle. Laurence arrived home baying for blood, and went through the roof when he saw her.

"I'll cut his fucking throat in the church," I heard him roaring in Claude's office. Neither of them noticed Olivia entering the apartment. Or passing through Trudi's room. Or diving off the balcony in a bikini, leaving a towel on the railing.

Olaf turned up for her funeral. I warned him about Laurence, and he smiled like a saint and said: "There's a God who steers our lives, no matter how we skid."

Or something like that. But he stayed clear of Laurence.

He stuck around town, but he didn't come home. He slept in his car. We met in parks, cafés. I begged him to go away. Laurence was after him, Claude as well no doubt. He smiled. One day he sang: *For you and I have a guardian angel . . .*

I thought, Jesus, he'll be telling me next he's found the mystery.

And sure enough, he sang: Ah, *sweet mystery of life, at last I've found thee . . .*

The next day was his twenty-first. We were in his car, heading out of the city. I talked again about danger.

"Every feather in my wings is counted," he said. "If I don't go now, I'll have to go later. If I go now, I won't have to go again. I'm ready."

And he burst into song:

> *Trailer for sale or rent;*
> *Rooms to let, fifty cents;*
> *No phone, no pools, no pets,*
> *I ain't got no cigarettes.*
> *Ah, but two hours of pushing broom*
> *Buys a eight by twelve four-bit room.*
> *I'm a man of means, by no means,*
> *King of the road.*

What happened next was Hollywood. He took my hand, spoke my name and said, "Goodbye, my love, you've been my only freedom."

"What are you talking about?" I asked him.

"Only with you have I been able to be free," he said, "because you're not in the script."

He braked, and undid my seat-belt, singing: *Keep your legs together coming home from my wake.*

Then he opened my door and pushed me out. Claude's BMW wasn't fifty yards behind him, with Laurence in the passenger seat. But Trudi's Volvo overtook them, and slammed into Olaf's U-turn. Claude skidded into them both and the lot of them went up in flames. An amazing spectacle.

The funeral arrangements were made by a Mr Armstrong, the Lethams' next of kin, from the North. The crowds were massive. TV crews jostled. Helicopters hovered. An amazing spectacle. I was hardly noticed.

I read *Hamlet* eventually. Amazing. I never came across anything like it. Disturbing too: if I'd read it earlier, could I have saved a few lives? But I don't have time for such speculation: between the baby and the business I've enough on my mind. Yes, I forgot to tell you: on my way to the morgue the morning after the accident, I dropped into school to pick up my Leaving Cert results. And as I was slitting open the envelope I remembered Olaf's last words, and it dawned on me that my period was overdue. So in the hospital I asked them to do a DNA test on Olaf; better do it now, I told them, than have to dig him up next May. So Mr Armstrong is still in the North; my Art inherited the empire.

If the lady is lying, she's an intruder, if she's telling the truth she's been written out, rendered invisible. Either way I empathize: I am the invisible intruder. In my family, my education, my work, my relationships, I have always felt: 'I have no right to be here', and at the same time: 'Nobody here even sees me.' No doubt the two notions are one. I know no-one more insecure. And insecure people can take terrible revenges. I'll say no more.

The silence is rest.

Enda Ring.

GODDESS

Dear Hayley,

You were the one pure passion of my life. From my thirteenth to my fifteenth year you reigned in my heart, my precious, my most secret secret. While my friends paired off and experimented, split up and sulked, I wrapped you in chaste embrace in a sphere apart. You were, to my chagrin, a year older than me, if not two, but by the time your films came round the gap had closed. In our bed – our chaste bed – I was, reassuringly, your senior.

For me you were peerless. I saw only some of your films, and have forgotten virtually everything except your face. I retain just one title: Whistle Down the Wind, in which you ministered to a criminal on the run in the belief that he was Jesus. But I remember my conviction that your genius equalled your beauty, matched your beauty, was your beauty. And how inexhaustible that was for my contemplation: the golden fleece of your hair, the kind bright eyes, the pert nose, the indescribably adorable lips . . . I sent you a fan letter via an agency and received a colour photo of you, signed 'To Enda, with much love, Hayley.' I sat at home from school for two days, turning it over and back like a three-card-trick man.

The end of our affair was sudden. I declined to attend a school hop – I just wasn't interested – and was ragged about it next day by a bunch of girls I was helping to clean up the hall. I responded impudently. They pushed me around a bit, and your photo fell out of my pocket. That's when they got nasty: they jeered me, knocked me to the ground, and stripped me naked. They tore the photograph in pieces and fed it to me, making me say to each morsel, 'I love you, Hayley.' After they'd left, I drew on some clothes and sat on the floor, in floods of tears. A girl approached, who had not been part of the attack. She apologised, helped me finish dressing, and comforted me. Before night fell I had had my first kiss, and acquired a new goddess, a new guilt.

Thanks to you I knew an intensity in my early teens. Here, for your contemplation, is another.

As a child I was addicted to stories. There were two beech trees in the Famine Field behind our house, and my father slung a hammock between them, where I could read in the summer holidays. Better still, he built a seat in one of them, and that's where I was happiest, pen in hand, spinning yarns in my little green world, with a few sheep munching below.

Two other things stand out in my childhood: my failure to get an answer when I asked why I had no brothers or sisters, and my mother's insistence that when I grew up I would not have to slave like my father. (Besides keeping sheep he owned an ash plantation, and made hurleys. She was – and still is – a teacher.)

My childhood ended when Father Drywood came to live with us; I was twelve. He was a distant English relative of my mother, and a former Jesuit. He had left the Order because he disapproved of its recent policies; he was now to be a theological consultant to the Irish hierarchy.

The day he arrived, I swear, I had read this passage in *Great Expectations*:

That was a memorable day to me, for it made great changes to me. But it is the same with any life. Imagine one selected day struck out of it, and think how different its course would have been. Pause you who read this, and think for a moment of the long chain of iron or gold, of thorns or flowers, that would never have bound you, but for the formation of the first link on one memorable day.

I knew that night that this had been such a day. He had some kind of magnetism. He was 50ish, thin and energetic, and he smiled a lot, but gravely. Life in our house became serious. There was Mass each morning, for myself and my mother. (The sheep began to require more of my father's time.) Weekly confession was established as the norm. There were little homilies, pious anecdotes, smiling exhortations to prayer and self-denial. (Within a month I had given up sugar. Three times he had me remove my sandals and stand for an hour in cold water; illogically, I transferred my self-pity to those scarred and weathered, faded, unoffending leather waifs.) There was always the awareness that in the next room, praying, thinking, writing, was, to quote my mother, 'a holy man of God'. I breathed more easily when he was away. The truth is, I feared him. He radiated some compelling force, and my answering antennae pulsated with a mild form of panic. The worst was knowing that he had yet to make a massively unpalatable demand, but that he would, and that I would submit.

I was fourteen when I overheard my mother ask him if God was calling me to the priesthood. My bowels liquefied.

"No, Gertrude, God has other plans for John," he answered.

What those plans were I would learn shortly after my Inter Cert. We were on top of our local mountains, the Slieve Blooms.

"Do you still want to be a novelist, John?" he asked me.

"Yes, Father," I said.

"There are enough stories already," he said, "and there's only one that matters. It was written, in one line, by your patron St John the Evangelist: *Et Verbum caro factum est, et habitavit in nobis: the Word was made flesh and dwelt amongst us* . . . We have enough storytellers, John. There's a higher calling: to *judge* stories in the light of the one true story."

"You mean be a literary critic, Father?" I asked.

"Not just any kind," he answered. "Gerard Manley Hopkins put his finger on it. In a letter he wrote from my old school, Stonyhurst, there's a line that's worth more than all his poetry. 'The only just judge,' he says, 'the only just literary critic, is Christ.' That's it. The true literary critic must have the mind of Christ. You must be *alter Christus, ipse Christus:* another Christ, Christ himself. You will enlighten the world if you are one with the Light of the world."

I was stirred. I was nervous, as always, but there was a thrill in this invitation to an Everest.

I had two more years before he dropped the bombshell. We were on the little hill of Knockeyon, overlooking Lough Derravarragh, where the children of Lir were turned into swans. He told me that celibacy was the shortest route to obtaining the mind of Christ; again he invoked the example of the Apostle John. I was stunned, struck numb and dumb.

"Pray about it," he said as we came down by the ruins of St Ion's chapel.

An old man passing pointed out a holy well and said, "The Salmon of Knowledge lived in that well till the clergy took over the country."

Father D, in civvies, chuckled; I couldn't even manage a smile.

All that summer I wrestled. I sought out the company of girls. Life with a woman could be beautiful, I decided. But that was precisely, I saw in prayer, why celibacy was the nobler option. I fought. But God always wanted what was hardest, and towards the end of the summer, I surrendered.

I enrolled for First Arts in UCG that autumn, and took English, French, German and Spanish. I had read the set texts in next to no time, and, under Father D's direction, I immersed myself in Homer, Virgil, Dante, Shakespeare and Goethe. On my weekends at home he tutored me in philosophy and theology; I had to learn to think with the mind of the Church. On the weekends too, as always, he heard my confession. I was, of course, he told me, free to confess to any priest, but he trusted that I would not avail myself of that freedom: for me, *he* was the Good Shepherd. He presented me with a book about Jesus: *This Tremendous Lover,* by a monk, Dom Eugene Boylan. On it he wrote, "Your sugarstick Christ will never nourish your soul."

My spiritual practices by now took two hours a day, but celibacy was the core of my religion; it crucified me. My contact with females was to be minimal and distant. Female beauty flowed around me like air, and I couldn't invite a girl for a coffee. I suffered agonies of scruples over thoughts, desires, 'motions of the flesh'. Repeatedly I confessed, repeatedly I received the standard counsel. He gave me a prayer for a crutch: the leper's confession of his rottenness, *Domine, si vis, potes me mundare; Lord, if you wish, you can make me clean.*

Towards Easter I became obsessed with a classmate because of her smile and her laughter. I wanted to talk to her. I tried never to be near her. I longed to stroke her hair; if our paths threatened to cross, I beat a retreat. The images I had to fight were hallucinatory; my scruples intensified. I humiliated myself: on my knees I told him her name: Melinda Molumby. Mercifully the exams supervened, and the summer somehow dissipated the obsession.

That became the pattern: routine distress alternating with exquisite torment. Obsessions with individuals aside, the struggle to 'guard the eyes and the heart' fuelled an infinity of dispiriting confessions. And yet, I *wanted* to win, I *wanted* to be *ipse Christus.*

My third year was spent in Paris; I took courses on nineteenth- and twentieth-century novels. My confessor was l'Abbé Duchesne, a fellow ex-Jesuit to whom Father Drywood has entrusted the care of my soul. I was happier that year than usual, until obsession struck in February. Sandrine Bouleau was her name; we attended the same seminars on the 'Catholic novel'. She took an interest in me, asked me questions about Ireland. I couldn't even look her in the eye. Seeing her as fulfilment and delight, I fled in terror; within days I was virtually demented. L'Abbé Duchesne asked me if I was sure I was able for what I'd taken on. I replied, "Of course, of course." There is in each of us, he said, a tiger; if we don't exercise him he will devour us.

One afternoon in March, crazed with temptation, suspecting I might be sick, I pushed aside Julien Green's *L'Autre*, and walked to the Louvre. There I found something more calming than aspirations: Georges de la Tour's penitent Magdalen. I was arrested by the perfect composition, and swept into rapt contemplation. Her illumined flesh, the skull on her lap, the darkness, the night-light flame, all hypnotised me. In the flame's still movement, I saw the Magdalen and myself being consumed by time, and was reconciled. An attendant tapped me on the shoulder; they were closing. I had been there an hour and a half. Back in my room, I finished Green's novel at a sitting. I abandoned my seminars, substituting visits to the Louvre. Though none matched the first, they helped me survive till the summer and my return to Ireland.

I took my BA the following year, and moved to Dublin to do a Master's. I began with brio, my only bookmark this quotation from Sir Thomas Browne:

I could be content that we might procreate like trees, without conjugation, or that there were any way to perpetuate the world without this trivial and vulgar way of coition; it is the foolishest act a wise man commits in all his life, nor is there any thing that will more deject his cool'd imagination, when hee shall consider what an odde and unworthy piece of folly hee hath committed.

Besides studying, I gave tutorials in French. I still travelled home on the weekends for my classes and confession with Father D. I ran into trouble before Christmas: infatuation with one of my students, Hazel Sweetman. I wanted to give up the tutorials, but Father D urged me to persevere, so as not to damage my prospects of a University career. Soon there was a second crisis. My awareness of my limitations was deepening. Reading certain critics, I knew I could never match them for erudition or insight. And some of my own teachers were in a league I could not aspire to. I began to regard Father D's ambitions for me as, at best, dubious. Great criticism, it seemed to me, had nothing to do with faith. No holiness could make up for lack of intellect. Anyway, I was as close to being *ipse Christus* as I was likely to sprout wings. And if the sanctity premise was false, then my celibacy was futile. We argued about knowledge, truth, insight, vision, then shelved the topic till my exams were over. By then, I was so agitated that he recommended a complete three-month break: I should even cut down on my spiritual practices.

I spent that summer touring in France, most of the time in a daze; on 14 September I awoke, in Colmar. I was in the Musée d'Unterlinden, face to face with Grünewald's Isenheim Altarpiece. The crucified Christ was astonishing, appalling. His trunk was discoloured and distorted. His feet crawled down the Cross like twisted roots. His crown of thorns was the nest of some terrible bird; he was the lacerated, oozing Tree of Life. I wept. And I saw in his sufferings a hideous image of my own. I wept more. And I boiled with murderous anger – at Father Drywood and all his empty promises, and to a lesser extent at my mother and her prim piosity. And I sloughed off my celibacy like a desiccated skin.

I was still gazing at that dishonoured flesh when a young woman approached and asked if I was all right. She had, she said, witnessed my distress; perhaps a cup of coffee would do me good. She had large dark eyes and long black hair, a thin face and a winning, impudent smile. I followed her. And I told her my story. Her name was Madeleine von Schädelberg: her father was German, but she, like her mother, was French. Her mother had committed suicide the previous year; she wasn't ready to talk about that yet. She was studying the history of art. Her father was a psychiatrist, and, as it happened, he would be attending a conference in Galway the following Easter. We agreed to stay in touch. Driving home I laughed aloud every few miles, savouring the champagne of freedom and relishing the promise of more. And I improvised celebratory songlines, random bursts of nonsense; one gem I remember was: 'Oh, blackguarded Greenwood Laddie is a cool clean shagger daddy.' I almost forgot to eat.

I drove straight to the West, and rented a cottage just outside Galway. I phoned my mother and told her I wouldn't visit home as long as there was dry rot in the house. I began to sign on, and settled down to study. I would not do a PhD; I wasn't ready to specialise. But as I explored a labyrinth in seven languages, one thread above all led me on: the figure of the Jew in European fiction.

Madeleine and I exchanged Christmas cards. But I was obsessed neither by her nor by anyone else that winter. In February she wrote to say she would accompany her father, and on the Tuesday before Easter I collected them from the train at Galway station. I delivered her father to his hotel, pointing out my cottage on the way; he was aware that Madeleine was to stay there. We were to meet up again on Saturday and they would tour for a week in a hired car. I was welcome to come along, he told me, if his daughter had not already driven me crazy.

Madeleine wished to see some of my Ireland, so in the morning we headed for the Slieve Blooms. We walked all day, discussing books, films, religion. Her background was agnostic. She asked me what I thought of *The Last Temptation of Christ*. I hadn't seen the film, but I was able to inform her that Christ did not desire Mary Magdalen: being God, he was free of that incompletion. (Her favourite film – she'd seen it six times – was *Wings of Desire*; it was about an angel who became a man and fell in love with a trapeze artist.)

My parents' house was empty: Father D had brought them to Medugorje; that night Madeleine slept in his room. She discovered his secret vice: 27 Zane Grey novels under the bed.

On Thursday I took her to Knockeyon, where I told her about the enchanted children and the banished salmon. We visited the Goldsmith country. I sang her 'Barbara Allen', which the writer had heard as a boy; she loved the true lovers' knot, – the rose and the briar entwining over their graves. We came home by Clonmacnoise. I explained that O'Rourke's Tower had been decapitated by lightning in 1135, and she said she'd love to see one that was entire.

"Tomorrow," I said, "I'll show you the tallest one in Ireland."

We took in Coole Park on our way and I brought her straight to the great copper beech, the autograph tree. With my arm through the protective railing, I traced the outlines of the signatures: GBS, John Millington Synge, WB Yeats . . . She withdrew my arm gently and said, "What a pity! Proclaiming every name except its own . . . And in a cage too . . . Sad."

At Kilmacduagh the round tower mesmerised her. She touched it, laid her cheek against it, stood back to contemplate it . . . I half expected her to levitate. She asked for details – date, function, height, angle of tilt – but seemed to be contemplating something more basic. There was a tension in her silence; eventually she sighed and rejoined me. A few steps took us to the Cathedral, where I began comparing two carvings of the Crucifixion: one tortured, one serene . . .

She cut me short – "Oh, haven't you had enough of blood and death?" – and walked out.

We crossed a field to O'Hyne's Monastery, and I showed her

the lepers' confessional: two well-spaced holes in a wall connected by a tunnel, enabling the diseased to be shriven without infecting their confessor. We took turns with mouth and ear, marvelling at the perfection of the sound.

"I have a confession to make," I heard suddenly . . . "I have loved you since Colmar, and I desire you now more every hour."

I stammered into the darkness, but she was beside me. We kissed, among the graves of the O'Shaughnessys and the Neylons and the Hyneses.

After that it was all ecstasy and exaltation. The Burren was a kaleidoscope of views and flowers and facts and legends and life: gentians and hermits and karst and mythical cows, and kisses and kisses and kisses as real as the rocks. Sunset found us at the Cliffs of Moher; as we lay entwined, our heads in dizzy space above toy waves, she shot a jet of spittle between my lips.

There was no question of sleep; we walked a green road and talked of our future. I could settle in France, she could move to Ireland, it was all the same, love would settle all, it would be bliss. As the east brightened, we drove to Poulnabrone to greet the sunrise. In the dolmen she kissed me with a new hunger.

"This is a tomb," I said.

"And a womb," she answered; "we're twins, about to be born."

She spread her cape on the ground and drew me down. It wasn't comfortable, it was cold, and I was clumsy, but we made what she called good love.

"I *know* you!" I exclaimed.

"The salmon is returned to the well," she said, laughing.

Then we emerged naked into the sun, to be ambushed by the most flamboyant rainbow in God's repertoire.

On the way to Galway I chattered non-stop; ten times she had to tell me to calm down. We lunched with her father, and he suggested a trip to Connemara. I drove, at random. Near Maam, I followed a signpost for Máiméan – St Patrick's well and bed; I'd never been there. When we began to walk the pilgrims' path, the doctor left us behind. I felt the lack of sleep. After half a mile, this thought shattered me: 'Madeleine von Schädelberg is Magdalen from the hill of the skull, i.e. Calvary; that makes me . . . that makes me *Ipse . . . Ipse . . .* '; I'm sorry, I'm not able to say the word. I began to shiver, and went quiet. As the climb grew steeper, I felt hot; I threw off my anorak, and later my sweater. Shortly afterwards we met the doctor coming down: we were almost there. Ahead of me was what looked like a tombstone. It wasn't; it was the tenth Station of the Cross: *Nochtar Íosa; Jesus is stripped of his garments.* I panicked: I was about to be crucified! Waves of cold flames ran up and down my brain; I expected the top of my skull to float off, like a fragment of burnt paper from a bonfire. I saw no holy well or saint's bed; I stumbled around the circle of the Stations: *Leagtar Íosa, An mac agus an mháthair . . . Mná caointe . . . Bás Íosa . . . Jesus falls, The Son and the Mother . . . Sorrowing women . . . Death of Jesus . . .* If it had to be, then so be it, I would go through with it . . . At the fourteenth station, I called to Madeleine and she came running.

"This is your place," I told her. "You must wait for me here, outside the tomb!"

"John," she said, "John, you're excited, you're overtired, you need rest."

Shocked back briefly into sanity, I took her hand and set off down the hill.

As we left her father at his hotel, I pointed to my muddy feet. "But Madeleine will wash them with her tears," I said, "and wipe them with her hair."

He looked at me for several seconds. "An odd sense of humour you have, Mr White," he commented.

In the cottage she sent me straight to bed. At the door of my bedroom I said, "This room too is a tomb and a womb. You must wait outside and watch over me. In the morning you will welcome me to my new life."

"Jesus Christ!" she said, then added, "I'll watch over you."

I didn't sleep. At 2.00 a.m. I phoned her father.

"I wish to congratulate you," I said, "on your daughter's vocation: the example of our love will redeem the world."

Within ten minutes he was at my door, bundling Madeleine into his car. I threw on shoes and rushed out.

"Wait inside, John," he said through the car window. "Help will be here very soon."

A new truth dawned on me. I put my mouth to his ear. "You Nazi bastard!" I hissed. "You crucified Jews in Buchenwald!"

And they shot off, Madeleine crumpled in her seat, a stricken swan.

I gave chase. I had no idea where they'd gone, and I found myself heading for Máiméan. I missed the turn, took a left and a right, ran out of petrol, freewheeled past a sign announcing County Mayo, and came to a stop outside a pub called The Larches. I entered through an open side-door and made my way to the bar. All I took was some chocolate. Then I staggered across country for several miles, convinced that a tiger was after me. Towards dawn I came on the remains of an ancient forest: thousands of grey-brown tree-stumps littering the plain like shattered tombstones. Sheep moped or lay around. I found a sheep's skull; I brandished it aloft and began to preach: "I am the Good Leopard! Confess to me and cleanse me from my spots!"

Around breakfast-time, two gardaí found me. I was stumbling naked by the shore of Lough Mask, crying out to the tree-stumps: "Arise, ye foolish virgins! Arise and take to your beds! Increase and multiply!"

In the pocket of my discarded pyjamas was an untouched bar of chocolate. Whole Nut.

In the hospital I informed everyone I would marry Madeleine. And I publicised my most recent discovery: there was no great writer named Black. Blake didn't count:

> Tyger, tyger burning bright
> In the forests of the night . . .

I sang 'Barbara Allen' loudly in the dayroom, and hummed it to myself in the ward:

Oh yes, I'm sick, and very very sick,
And death is on me dwellin';
The better of love I never shall be
If I can't have Barbary Allen . . .

They grew, they grew, so very very high
Till they could grow no higher;
And there they grew to a true lover's knot,
For the rose grew round the green briar.

Under my mattress I found the final page of a book, *The Green Child*. It excited me intensely: two lovers united in death, turning to crystalline stone. I asked around; it was nobody's. I was convinced it was a message from Madeleine.

Father Drywood called to see me. I chased him, shouting: "Run before me, Satan", and wishing I had one of my father's hurleys. The rest of that month is a blur.

When I was discharged, I half-expected to find Madeleine waiting in the cottage. I found this letter.

Dear John,

I know you will have been in hospital, and I hope you begin to be better. I have done you much harm, I made you to go too quickly. It is best that we do not contact ourselves more. It seems, alas, that our love was a holidays adventure. I thought I was the trapeze girl and you were the angel; it was a dream. As my father says, it is necessary to keep the head cold. Do not lose hope. Our happiness together had a sense, you must believe it. Our little corner of paradise can be a golden memory that gives us courage on the way. Thank you and good-bye.

With affection,

Mad.

P.S. I'm sorry.

143

I fell apart. I bawled like a baby. I wanted to run back to the hospital: it might make the letter unhappen. I phoned my mother. She was about to set out to visit me for my birthday; I had forgotten it. When she arrived I was still clutching the incredible page. I wept uncontrollably again. She said the best place for me was at home with her; I said not unless the adversary was evicted. Impossible. When she'd left, I unwrapped her gift. A bonsai beech tree in full leaf. I lost control. I raged against my rearing: I was a bonsai man. I had spent my life in a playpen, and hadn't even been allowed to play. I tore the tree from its tray and beat it against the wall; the clay that fell from the roots was Father Drywood's brain. I stood the tree in the grate and set fire to the roots; the shrivelling leaves were von Schädelberg's hair and beard.

I wrote to Madeleine, pleading for another chance. Impatient, three days later I wrote again. And then again, and again, every day for over a week. And my letters drifted back, one a day, like slow snowflakes floating through my door. I lay in bed, I scarcely ate, I couldn't read. Even my power to hate lost its edge. My mother came and went; fresh sheets and cheery cuisine changed not a thing. All summer I floundered in a pitch-filled pit. Was life worth living? my shrink asked, on one of my weekly visits. Not this life, I told him.

Slowly, I surfaced. Food had a taste again. I could follow print again. The effort of a walk verged on pleasure. And my anger reawakened, yawning: Father D I wanted dead, the doctor I wanted to murder – without exertion. I brooded with new energy on Madeleine, irreplaceable, flawless, unique. I spoke to her. I wrote – an interminable unsent letter. I dreamed: I had a beautiful future behind me, why not a golden past ahead?

And autumn became winter, became spring. There was no urgency about the Jews in others' fictions: I knew I would never write a book. I was a reader, a bookworm getting the name of being odd. And two years passed.

My mother phoned some time last February. Father D was in hospital with cancer; he had weeks to live: would I visit him? I would not. She tried again around Patrick's Day; he had particularly asked for me. Let him ask, I said. He did, and I relented.

He was at home by now, being nursed. He didn't hear my knock or notice me enter. I saw a skeleton sitting up, gazing out the window and quietly *singing* . . .

> *Don't sit under the apple-tree*
> *With anyone else but me,*
> *Anyone else but me,*
> *Anyone else but me;*
> *Don't sit under the apple-tree*
> *With anyone else but me,*
> *Till I come marching home.*

Then he saw me.

"John," he said, "forgive me. I have wronged you. I abused my power. I am offering God my death, asking Him to lead you soon to the woman who will share your life."

At his funeral I overheard a nurse say: "He was a saint, that man. He suffered something fierce, and he wouldn't take morphine. He said the only painkiller he wanted was his crucifix."

And I heard a Jesuit remark: "Great man for the imagination, old James. He was as much a consultant to the hierarchy now as I'm the Cardinal."

My obsessions became more focused after this. Madeleine's father had a monopoly on my anger, and my conviction grew that she was the one destined for me. I decided that she had to be confronted. I needed to knock on her door and make her see sense. If I failed, I could let her father have it.

I drove, rehearsing my case for four days. On a Friday

afternoon I was outside the right village, crawling along the right road, looking for a house named Les Cerisiers. When I saw two cherry-trees flowering behind a hedge, something exploded in my stomach; I passed two other houses before I stopped, and for ten minutes I considered aborting my mission. Then, in a kind of trance, I walked towards the clouds of flowers.

It was the swing I saw first, the movement of the rope between the cherries. Then, simultaneously, Madeleine, gently pushing, and the child: a two-year-old red-haired replica of my father.

"You should have told me," I said eventually.

"That's what my father thought," she answered. "But I didn't want complications."

"That child," I said, "is another reason we should be together. We're meant for each other, Madeleine."

"Oh, when will you face facts?" she asked. "We are not together and we will not be together. While you hope the impossible, your life wastes away."

"The child needs a father," I said.

"He will have one," she retorted. "On 24 June he will acquire a father. If you wish to meet my fiancé you can call back in one hour."

That shook me. I saw limbs that weren't mine playing around her body, and it was unbearable; I had no desire to meet their owner.

"What's the boy's name?" I asked.

She had him in her arms at this stage, nuzzling him. "David," she answered. "And for all we know he might be the Messiah. Isn't that right, pet?"

She kissed him on the forehead and let him down; he waddled off towards the house.

"What sort of talk is that?" I asked.

"I'm joking, of course," she said. "But he *is* Jewish."

I gaped at her.

"Jewishness comes from the mother," she said. "And my mother was Jewish."

"Your mother?"

"Yes. She was a survivor of Belsen; she was fifteen when it ended, and for some reason she stayed on in Germany. She attended my father with depression a few years later, and they married within months. A great scandal, of course. He was ostracised: by his colleagues, his family, his class, and lots of upstanding Germans. Which is why they moved to France. But her depression never really lifted . . . He feels he failed her. I think he sometimes feels he was unwise, trying to carry that burden."

I could say nothing. I wondered if I should ask to see the old man, but I didn't feel up to it. And then he strode out of the house, with David in his arms. He was startled to see me, as I was by the warmth of his greeting.

"He knows," Madeleine told him.

"Good," he replied, "I'm glad. No doubt you'll arrange for further visits to this little man. I don't know what the law says about these things, but I trust you'll work out something sensible between you."

And after a minute of small talk he said, "Wave day-day to Uncle John, David." (I'm translating, of course.)

And David – and his grandfather – waved day-day to Uncle John. And Uncle John waved day-day to David and his grandfather as they retreated. And then he waved day-day to Madeleine as well and made for the gate, saying, "I have to go away and think about all of this," and banged his knee off the corner of a wheelbarrow, drawing blood.

I was half-way to the car when I realised: I hadn't kissed my son or held him or spoken to him or heard a word from his mouth. I considered going back, but was too embarrassed. And that's when I realised I didn't know how to be a father.

I drove in a daze of confusion. That night I checked into a hotel in Bruyères; I signed the register like an automaton, and fell asleep exhausted. Towards morning I had this dream. The Famine Field. The beech trees. By the tree with the seat, Madeleine, her back to me. Studying my initials: JEW (E for Emmanuel). She turns to me, turning to stone. On her breast a yellow star. David I see then, swinging between the trees. He's twelve. The swing is a little upturned rainbow. "Father," he says, "Father, your father is no father."

I awoke, understanding. I would make my father pay for having failed me.

I arrived home the day after his funeral. He'd had a heart attack while delivering a lamb. The farm and the hurley-making business were mine, my mother told me, hoping I'd stay. Within a month I had sold the business and the sheep, and let most of the land. I bought the cottage in Galway and sent Madeleine – in time for her wedding – a first contribution towards David's rearing. (He'll be seeing more of Uncle John, but not just yet: some wounds have still to heal.)

I'm learning to turn my attention to other women. I've made some friends: Lorelei Lillis, Orla Pine, Cherry O'Carroll . . . Oh, and guess who's back in town: Melinda Molumby, fresh from Ethiopia! She's been working closely with some Falashas who missed the airlift to Israel during the famine, and has her very own black baby (Oasis) to prove it. Appalling things have happened to her, and she laughs herself sick as she tells them.

What about love? I'm waiting for the miracle. Will it strike through the intercession of St James Drywood, impostor and martyr? I do not lose hope. For me too, perhaps, some woman is waiting.

Meanwhile, I worm my way through more books, more determined than ever never to be a critic. Of late, however, in my gut, I have detected, fermenting, the makings of . . . a novel! But I shall nip it in the bud and strangle it at birth and give it a hasty burial in an unmarked grave. (How could I not distrust fiction, having myself been taken – to my ruination – for a fiction, and an angelic one at that?) Anyway, there are too many novels already, and we should cut down on cruelty to trees. I speak as the owner of a wood: last June I planted the entire Famine Field with young beeches. I renamed it Buchenwald one black day, feeling bitter towards Madeleine, angry with the world and disgusted with myself. I've since scrapped that for something less dramatic: Kylenalour. The wood of the books . . . The church of the books . . . The graveyard of the books . . . The lepers' wood . . . The lepers' church . . . The lepers' graveyard . . .

A stew of disparate ingredients, this.

The strangest thing I've ever witnessed was a tug-o'-war between a young couple on the edge of the cliffs of Moher: he was trying to drag her over, she was trying to pull him back. Result? A draw. The last thing he did was to spit at her.

Three years ago I went on a skite and ended up in Buchenwald; the name had always haunted me. Two obscenities on display made me retch. One was a large metal wheelbarrow for transporting dead and dying; it had a hole in one corner for blood to drain off. The other was a mound of children's shoes, conscientiously tied in pairs. It was these that decided me to go straight home. At the exit I met an elderly couple entering; they were holding hands and weeping quietly. They were French Jews who had met and fallen in love in the camp; it was their first visit back. He was a cellist, she a psychiatrist; they lived in Épinal. They were ten years younger than my parents would have been.

I worship trees: for every book I read I plant one. (Well, I did, for a while, two decades ago.) For years I grew bonsai trees. I know the Burren like the back of my hand, and Kilmacduagh, and Máiméan. My favourite painters are Grünewald and de la Tour. I've read all the works of Zane Grey. I love European films.

I have chased sheep on the shores of Lough Mask. I have sung ballads in psychiatric wards. I have never committed myself to celibacy. I can't stand chocolate. I have never loved a Frenchwoman: my obsession for twenty years has been an Anglo-Irish lesbian with a double-barrelled name. I have had relationships with a number of others. I am married.

Was there ever a Father Drywood in my life? Pass.

John White will accomplish nothing while his mother lives.

I never tell my children stories.

*An old woman I know as 'Danny's granny' said to me today:
'The best thing to do with shit is use it as fertilizer.'*

One can take on too much.

I would love to write a book I would love to have written.

Yours nostalgically,

Enda Ring.

SCOFFER

26 August

Dear Severin Lafayette,

28 years on, your 25-year-old self is sharper in my memory than in your own. You can have no idea of the effect you had on me. (I know no better example of how a gesture or remark can, unknown to one, turn another life upside down.)

No doubt you don't remember the bus-trip we made through Alsace-Lorraine with twenty other students from that course at the Council of Europe. (You can hardly have forgotten the course, if only because of Conchita.) And I don't expect the name Enda Ring rings any bells for you.

Conchita came from Córdoba, and from our first evening I had my shy eye on her. On the Sunday we were the only two from the course to attend Mass in the Cathedral, but I gave her a headstart when it ended, and kicked myself as I watched her hair, arse, missal and legs dance their way back to the Hotel Pax. And now, at the back of the bus, I chewed half a biro flat as I tried not to hear you regaling a Finn and two Cypriots with the story of how you had seduced Conchita the night before. (She was sitting near the driver, her head in a book.)

Our first stop was in some medieval town. As soon as I got off

the bus I saw Conchita walking away from the group. I hurried
after her and asked her if she'd like to join me for a coffee. She
said 'Go and fuck yourself, Paddy.' I rejoined the others. At the
door of a tavern the guide pointed out a stone carving that depicted
Christ turning water into wine. No-one made a comment, but your
lips formed your trademark smirk, you tilted your blond head
back, and you rocked with a pompous, ponderous laughter that
I have heard again every time I have heard the words 'Cana' or
'Geneva'. No-one commented on your reaction either, but at that
moment I understood, I saw, how absurd the miracle story was,
how unbelievable any 'miracle'. Not my patchy reading, in later
years, of Darwin, Nietzsche, Marx or Freud; not the influence of
Jews, Muslims or Buddhists, pious or lapsed; not all the clerical
scandals imaginable, could have accomplished what you did in
three seconds: you took a full bucket – well, half-full anyway –
and emptied it with a flick of your wrist.

Perhaps you did me a favour. I don't know. But what I have
resented ever since, and still resent, is the condescension, the
contempt with which you did it. I hate mockery. And I hate your
smug, superior smirk. I wish I could see you yoked to the bitch
whose voice you are about to hear.

I was married to David Burley; that tells you a good deal of my
story.

I was doing my H Dip when I met him; he was still at the
College of Art. I had heard of him before that, of course, and his
outrageous practical jokes. I remember two things from the party
where I first saw him: the energy of his conversation and laughter,
and the liberties he took with several women. When he turned to
me I gave him a look of ice and he found some other victim. A
week later he appeared at my door with a load of vegetables, two
bottles of wine and a boyish grin; before I could get my breath
back he was cooking dinner. He tried to get me into bed, of
course, but I said, "I'll sleep with you when I'm married to you,"

and we enjoyed our first real laugh together. I liked him better than I let on.

My life progressed as planned: after my Dip I got a job in my old school, lived with my parents and helped them at weekends with the horses. Then David showed up, gave me a painting of a flying blue foal, and asked me to marry him. I refused, of course, but he returned three times in a month with new versions of the flying foal, and I said yes. He had just had a successful exhibition and my parents were satisfied that he had a future.

My brother Fergal almost wrecked our engagement party: he announced that he was joining the Benedictines and sent my sister Louise, who was fourteen and crazy about him, into hysterics. Fergal was always a bit odd: his big thing was the history of art, and he spent his summers in galleries and museums. Anyway, he did become a monk and wrote books about God and the modern artist. When he saw my four blue foals he said they showed promise.

David and I honeymooned in Spain. The physical side of things I found . . . difficult, but David was all gentleness at first. Then something in the place got to him: he enthused with vehemence about the landscape, the light, the sunflowers, the white villages, the herds of bulls . . .

"I want to paint all this!" he shouted one day, repeatedly. He reminded me of a little boy in a tantrum, but he made me a tiny bit afraid.

We were in Seville for Semana Santa. On Good Friday we watched the procession from the balcony of our bedroom. I must admit it disgusted me: the bleeding Christs, the wild piety, the penitents scourging themselves, the blood . . . Even the smell of orange blossom became tainted. David watched in a trance. When it was over he drew me to the bed, tore off my clothes and proceeded to devour me; he seemed surprised that I was not enjoying it. I put it down to excitement, saw in it the energy of a hyperactive child. It didn't happen again, but a few nights later in

Granada he announced that he was coming in the back door. I didn't know what that meant, but I soon learned, and I didn't like it; there was no repeat of that prank either.

Back home, I taught, he painted – jumbles of objects mainly. In July I discovered I was pregnant, and for safety's sake I refused any physical advances. As I grew big he asked me to pose for him. I agreed, on condition that I wouldn't be recognisable. For days I sat, bored. He finished two huge canvases before he showed me anything. The first was all bridles and saddles and stirrups arranged any old way, no trace of a human figure.

"When you've absorbed that," he said, "I'll show you the other."

The other was a pregnant tigress, sleeping on a little girl's bed. I didn't appreciate the waste of my time or his idea of a joke, but I was too preoccupied with the imminent birth to make a scene.

I expected fatherhood to bring him some maturity. It didn't; he would grow bored of Paul after five minutes and retire to his studio. He hired a model; she looked like a hippy and a hussy, and after three days I could smell her off him. I ran her and told him he was barred from my bed for a month; he laughed at that. That night, sober as a judge, he forced himself on me and made me pregnant again.

He had an exhibition in Limerick shortly after. At the opening he met a woman called Grace Mills, the most beautiful woman I've ever seen: pale complexion, full lips, huge olive eyes, short dark hair, perfect poise, oozing elegance and class. She expressed interest in one particular painting, one I hadn't seen till that evening: me eight months pregnant, stretched out on a turfbank, drinking a pint of porter; he made her a present of it. In no time they were having an affair. He spent nights, weekends, away; he came and went with the bravado of a tipsy schoolboy.

He grew tired of her in time to pay some attention to Brian's birth. I hoped we might become a normal family, but he was off again before the child had cut a tooth. He had a fling with the local judo instructor's wife and got a broken nose for it; he wasn't long recovered when he moved in with a separated woman and her four kids in Tullamore. I kept taking him back because I felt he would come to his senses and realise who loved him. When I took a group of fifth years to Paris at Easter I brought him along to replace a sick teacher; he got one of the girls pregnant. There was hell to pay; luckily she miscarried. I told him he was on his last chance.

Early that summer he disappeared to Dublin with my sister, Louise. She was eighteen; she'd been in my French class three weeks before. I took the children to West Cork and watched the first man walk on the moon and hoped the scandal would have evaporated by the end of the holidays. But in September they were still together; I had to face lowered eyes from colleagues and sniggers from students. Fergal got leave to go and talk with Louise; he was wasting his breath. I wrote to the pair of them, saying I forgave them and was ready for a fresh start. Silence. I got on with my life; people commended my dignity.

Louise left him two years later, when he was charged with raping a heavily pregnant woman. At the trial he grinned at me; he could have been an altar-boy caught drinking the wine. He pleaded guilty and got six years; he served four.

I visited the prison once a month, though he never agreed to see me. On my second visit I brought watercolours and drawing-paper; he sent me a note telling me to wipe my . . . bottom with them. It was the only note I got from him, although I left him a little letter every time. In the four years I missed one visit, when the boys had measles.

I had an unpleasant little experience after one visit, in the third year. I was sitting alone in the lounge of a hotel, having a cup of tea and a cream bun, when a well-dressed portly older man, who looked vaguely familiar, approached me. He asked me if I'd care to spend an hour with him in room 104. I lunged at him with my fork and rammed the prongs into his ample belly. He yelped and staggered out, backwards and bent double. For a few days I regretted having lost my dignity, until I saw his death announced on TV; he was a former showband leader who'd created a stir in the 60s by abandoning his wife for some young bimbo.

Fergal lost an arm in an accident about this time; he was so cheerful you'd think he'd lost a glove.

"If a monk can't know when a loss doesn't matter, who can be expected to?" was his comment. He was a great comfort to me during those years.

I was at the door of the prison the morning of David's release, but he wouldn't come out of his cell until I'd left. I sent him a note saying I wanted to bring him home and help him heal. He scrawled on the back of the note, "*Physician, heal thyself,*" whatever that was supposed to mean.

I lost touch with him. There were occasional sightings, snatches of rumours: he was dealing in drugs, he was pimping, he was making pornographic videos; he was never painting. Silence for a year or so, then someone ran into him in Málaga; he was living with some 40-year-old woman and screwing every 20-year-old in reach; not a word about painting all of Spain.

The next event is history: David, on his first weekend back in Ireland, at a party in the Ambassador's residence, getting off with the Ambassador's daughter, strangling her in her bed after sex. Everyone agreed she was a younger version of me. He was arrested in a cinema, watching *A Man For All Seasons*. He got life, of course.

Again the visits began, and the letters, but only every six or eight weeks. He never saw me, but soon asked for paints and canvases, specifying large sizes. I brought supplies on each visit. The assistant governor told me he had gone totally silent and was painting like a madman. I asked to see the paintings but he said:

"I don't think you want to see them, missus; I'm keeping them for the psychiatrist."

They were difficult years. Mummy died. Brian had several

breakdowns. Paul married an unsuitable girl. Daddy was
crotchety with arthritis and loneliness. We never heard from
Louise; she was in Hamburg or Amsterdam and gone all New
Agey. In my mid-40s I felt already old.

On 1 April 1990, David was moved to hospital with a heart
attack. He was dead by the time I arrived; Fergal had been with
him at the end. I asked him what had passed between them, but
he didn't hear me. I didn't cry when I saw David's body. "Like
Shakespeare, only blond," I remember thinking, and suddenly I
felt ten years younger. "There's life after David," I heard myself
repeating.

After the cremation I went with Fergal to the prison. The
governor told me David had broken his silence a week before, to
say that the paintings were for me. I almost cried a little. He
brought us to a store-room; there were 153 canvases, he told us,
and proceeded to display them. The most recent was still wet; if
showed a clown holding his eyes in his outstretched hands, while
black blood streamed from the sockets. I was horrified, but it was
the mildest. There were two rats copulating in a skull with hair
like mine. There was a woman giving birth to twin baby skeletons.
There were close-ups of penises and vulvas and anuses, some of
them disfigured by disease. There was a crucified woman with no
blood from the nailmarks, and a snake slithering from her vagina
with a wasp-covered apple in its mouth. There was a circle of
thirteen skeletons, each one penetrating the one in front with a
lurid livid pink and purple penis. There were two babies in a
baptismal font, being eaten by a huge blue stallion with an erection.
There were two putrefying corpses copulating in a coffin, and the
face of the woman was mine . . . I reeled from the room, found
the nearest toilet and threw up. When I returned I saw Fergal
hadn't missed me; he was engrossed in conversation with the
governor. I closed my eyes and let them continue the sewer-crawl
without me; at one point I heard Fergal say "Bosh". I arranged
with the governor to have the lot delivered to me.

I put on a pair of old leather gloves, and dragged those paintings face down to the end of the garden. For good measure I added to the pile the four blue foals from the attic. I threw on three gallons of petrol, struck a match and watched until all was ashes.

Fergal called a week later.

"Those paintings should be in a monastery," he said, "In the mountains, where only dedicated pilgrims can see them."

I told him what I had done. He was speechless for more than a minute; I saw two or three changes of colour in his face.

"How important were they?" I asked him.

"Gauguin . . ., Van Gogh . . ." He could hardly get the words out . . . "That important . . . maybe . . . Who knows?"

He got up to go.

"He hated me because I loved him," I said.

"It isn't always easy to tell love from hate," he answered. "Forgiveness can be a form of punishment. Bitterness can mask repressed affection."

We've had virtually no dealings since that day.

Paul is managing the home place since Daddy died two years ago. Louise showed up for the funeral: telepathy, she said. She dropped hints about staying at home, but I discouraged her; she's got a fairly serious drug problem, and even if she'd never stolen David, I'd have washed my hands of her; there's nothing I could do for the likes of her. I've enough on my hands with Brian. He was talking for a while about becoming a painter; you can guess how fast I put my foot down about that. A writer he says he wants to be now, and he spends his time scribbling; accounts of his breakdowns, as far as I can make out. It won't get him far, God knows, but it keeps him busy and quiet.

Some months ago a young woman came to interview me about David; she was researching a book on contemporary Irish artists. She had located all the paintings from his two exhibitions, and wanted to know if there was anything from more recent times; she predicted that his work would fetch "very significant" prices fairly soon.

Not long after that I had a visit from Grace Mills. She had been too embarrassed to come and see me earlier, but her meeting with the young researcher had decided her. She was most sympathetic, and she cried a bit while talking about David, and she hugged me and asked me to forgive her. Then she offered to give me the painting that David had made her a present of. I declined, because I couldn't have the thing in the house, but I suggested that, if she liked, she could have the ownership transferred to me, while continuing to look after it in her own home. She was delighted with the idea and hugged me again, and her solicitor drew up the agreement within days.

What can I say to finish? I think I got a raw deal from God. I know there's heaven, but I think there should be a way of getting justice in this life too. And . . . well, no, in fact . . . it isn't as simple as that . . . To tell the truth, I get bouts of doubts sometimes, when I *quake* at the notion of justice.

She killed him, didn't she? Just as clearly as she killed the bloke in the hotel. Unwilling to see her husband as a man – always a little boy, wasn't he? She drove him to what he did. And her dignity, her respectability . . . it makes me puke. The country was full of women like her when I was growing up. My mother was one of them. And since my father wriggled out from under her early on, I got the brunt of her attentions. 'I'll cut it off!' she warned me once, when she found me playing with myself. She was brandishing a carving-knife. I was three and a half. I tried for years to persuade myself that she'd said: 'I'll cut the turf' – there wasn't a bog within twenty miles of us – or 'I'll gut a toff' or 'you'll get a cough' or . . . or something, anything else. But I knew, and I feared and resented her ever after. The next time I felt anything like love for her, she was stretched in her coffin. So I know where this story originates: for murder read emasculation. Thankfully not all women were like that. I had the good fortune later to get to know (slightly) an old woman named Tessie, the best and kindest person I've ever met. She phoned last night, as it happens, and said, à propos of nothing in particular: 'Pretend you don't exist: it'll only be a teensy-weensy lie', and, at another stage: 'In a black pit you'll see a light shone on you far quicker than if you were stretched in the sun.' Ah yes, but who knows if any light will ever shine? Perhaps she meant me to pass her words on to some reprobate like you.

Yours resentfully,

Enda Ring.

SAINT

16 August

Dear Tessie the Trolley,

I never gave you a word beyond 'Morning' or 'See you'. And will I tell you why? Because I resented your goodness; you were the nearest thing to a saint I ever met.

Things I could see about you that summer in the supermarket: you were 65, maybe 70; you could push only three trolleys at a time, stopping for breath every twenty yards; you were so slight that I wondered you could push any; in the presence of any person you had a permanent smile; you were a most patient listener: when that great bore, the boss of the meat section, assailed you with his fulminations against corruption in business and politics, you smiled, nodded, and occasionally interjected, 'We'll pray for them.' (You once said more, interrupting a tirade against the travellers: 'How can you talk like that, John? You'll be facing your God, all naked, in a few short years.' He was talking to you again next day.)

Things I heard about you: you were paid a pittance; recovering trolleys that had strayed, you saved the management ten times your wages; with your smile you could get the roughest man or boy to rescue a trolley from the canal; you were a daily communicant and you knelt before the tabernacle for an hour each evening; you

165

lived in a council house with a crotchety brother, for whom you cooked and cleaned; you were a solid member of the Union; you spent Sundays with traveller families, telling the children stories and teaching them to read; you had been fourteen years in English hospitals with TB, and a series of operations had left you with half a lung; you were a native Irish speaker.

Some months after I had returned to college, I heard that you'd been raped and badly beaten. Let me confess now one of the things in my life of which I am most ashamed: before I felt shock or sympathy at the news, I sniggered at the incongruity. It was said you knew your attacker but wouldn't reveal his identity, for fear some of your friends might do him in. Within a week you were back pushing trolleys, your face still purple and yellow. People said you'd never retire.

The last time I saw you was early on a September Sunday morning. I had got the results of my MA on the Friday, and been plunged into anger and despair. I had been awarded a pass. I could not enrol for a PhD, I could not get a scholarship to an American university, I could not look forward to an academic career, I would have to be somebody ordinary. I went for a walk before anyone was up, and headed for the docks, thinking about throwing myself in. Melodramatic? Well, people do that sort of thing. Anyway, I wasn't fully decided, but I was thinking about it. And then I saw you on the Dock Road, carrying two large black and brown suitcases. One at a time, of course: you'd carry one maybe twenty yards, set it down and go back ten yards for the other, carry that one twenty yards, leapfrogging the first one, and so on. You were like something out of Beckett, if you ever heard of him. God knows how long you'd been at it, or how far more you had to go. Were you moving house maybe, or bringing tinned food to the travellers? I watched you for some minutes as one might study a strange insect; it never occurred to me that I could offer help. Then I turned away and made for the city centre.

Believe it or not, I often wondered where you'd die. On the steps of the Augustinian church? In the muck of a traveller encampment? At a Union meeting? In hospital? In the street? In your bed, with your brother complaining about having to boil his own egg? None of the above, of course; you gave us all a surprise: in a cinema seat, having sat, alive and dead, through 40 hours of a Laurel and Hardy marathon. Did you die laughing?

Passers-by took your funeral for a traveller affair; your few neighbours were seen holding their noses. The supermarket was not represented, and resentment still kept me away. Guilt drove me eventually to the cemetery; I hadn't a clue where you were buried, but in no time I located the spot: a supermarket trolley stood right on your grave. I came near to praying.

The trolley – I don't know whether you're aware of these things – was removed by your employers, but was quickly replaced. This was repeated a few times, so they gave up the fight and it's still there. I gather it's renewed each year on your anniversary, and it's the only memorial you have. Decades after your death, it's part of the cemetery's folklore, pointed out to tourists visiting the graves of the famous.

I have a story for you, Tessie; I hope you'll take the time to have a look at it.

I sat down to 4,000 meals in boarding school; at the most memorable one I ate nothing. It was in my final year, in 1964. We were all – 150 of us – standing silently in the refectory, facing the crucifix at the upper end, waiting for our woodwork teacher, Father Lyons, to say grace, when he asked the boy beside me – Purcell – why he was smiling. Purcell said he wasn't smiling. Lyons repeated his question, Purcell gave the same answer. Lyons shouted, "Purcell, get out!"

Purcell stayed put; Lyons repeated the order; Purcell didn't budge. Then Lyons said, "Do I have to go down and put you out? You have five seconds. If I have to lay my consecrated hands on you, I won't be responsible for what I do to you."

Purcell stood his ground. Lyons came striding down and grabbed Purcell's jumper. Purcell held on to the table. Lyons punched him on the side of the head and knocked him over; then he picked him up by the hair and pushed him towards the door. Purcell resisted, and Lyons went wild entirely; he punched and kicked and shoved and shouted. He'd push his glasses up with his left hand and flail out at Purcell's head with his right, then he'd lift his cassock and kick him in the legs and back. I'm not making this up; this happened. Purcell cooperated no more than a sack of spuds, he had to be kicked the whole way. It seemed to take an eternity, but finally he was in the corridor. Lyons slammed the door and resumed his position to say grace; his hands were trembling so much that he wasn't able to bless himself. It was at that moment that I decided to become a priest.

I entered the seminary the following September, and my biggest shock was to find Purcell there as well. We hung around together, and we teamed up with three other lads: Gallagher, Clancy and Gavin. (I'm Burke, by the way.) We discussed everything endlessly: our lectures, our lecturers, the seminary regime, the state of the country and the world. We became increasingly critical of the setup, and one day in spring when we were sitting beside the river, Gallagher said, "Let's face it, lads, we're not going to stick it out here; why not get out now instead of wasting more months or years?"

After a long silence, three of us said he was right; Gavin said nothing.

Then Gallagher said: "Well, since we won't be taking a vow of chastity, I suggest we each take another vow." He produced a pack of cards and said that each had a different vow written on it; we would each blindly choose one.

Clancy went first; he picked the knave of diamonds and read out: "*I will be myself.*"

Purcell pulled out the two of clubs and read: "*I will be a friend to my enemy.*"

I was next; I got the seven of spades and read: "*I will be a pilgrim in my own place.*"

That gave me a start: if I'd had to state my main complaint

with the seminary, I'd have said: "I'm fed up being told in such detail what to believe; a man should be able to learn all he needs to know in the place where he's born, by observing what goes on around him."

Gallagher offered the cards to Gavin; Gavin said, "Include me out: I'm staying," but Gallagher shuffled the cards and dropped one at Gavin's feet; it was the king of hearts and it read: "*I will put love before law.*"

Then Gallagher chose for himself; it was the Joker, and he read: "*I will go round the world for sport.*" Then he bent the pack in his right hand and shot the remaining cards into the river; he said, "There go all our other possible lives."

I thought what he had done was a pity; the cards were old and the writing was a perfect copperplate in ink that had faded to bronze.

I came home, and in 30 years I've never been more than ten miles away. I started working the farm with my father, and when he died the following year, I was left the house and the 36 acres. Farming wasn't my first priority: that thing about being a pilgrim stuck with me. I wanted to be humble and to learn. I listened to the land and the lake, I paid attention to everything. I studied my animals. (In the seminary we were told man was a rational animal; a useless definition since we didn't know what an animal was.) I learned from other creatures too – crows, snails, spiders – and from all kinds of plant-life. I wasn't long realising there was a universe in my fields. I watched the weather, I asked old people about cures, I helped in an archaeological survey of the parish. I wasn't a great socialiser, but I tried to be a good neighbour and to respond to needs: I even kicked football for the local team a few times and gave swimming lessons to youngsters.

My closest friend was my nearest neighbour, Joe King. Joe had an unfortunate accident the year my father died. There was a sports day in the village and he was measuring the distance for the javelin. When his own son, Lar, threw, Joe got distracted or misjudged the distance, and he got the javelin in the private parts. I can hear the youngsters laughing yet. He spent only a few nights in hospital, but within a month he had a bad back and he could neither stand nor sit in comfort. But he never lost his smile. What bothered him most was that he wouldn't be able to fish. So I built him a special padded seat and installed it in his boat, and whenever he wanted to go on the lake I would row him out. I never fished myself, I preferred to watch him and chat.

The year after Joe's accident a young lad of fifteen called Malachy Page came looking for summer work. I took him on. He was a grand cheerful young lad, always singing. He didn't like milking the cows in the byre, he'd bring them out to the haggard and milk them beside the water-tank; I can still see him lifting his head from the shorthorn's flank and singing:

> *She wore an itsy-bitsy teeny-weeny*
> *Yellow polka-dot bikini*
> *That she wore for the first time today,*

and then laughing and saying: "Wouldn't she be nicer wearing nothing at all?"

One evening in August he didn't come in to his tea; I went looking for him and found him in the haybarn, hanging. I thought for a second he was playing a joke, but he wasn't. A line from his song kept going over and over in my head:

> *She was afraid to come out of the water . . .*
> *She was afraid to come out of the water . . .*

Even while taking him down I was trying to think of the next line. When I got over the shock I cursed myself for not noticing whatever must have been bothering the poor kid; I punished myself by fasting until Christmas. And a few evenings a week I would climb Hunter's Hill, the highest point of the parish, and sit for ages brooding over the lake.

"Why is there so much suffering in the world?" I asked Joe one day.

He said, "You might as well ask why there's oxygen in air: it's one of the ingredients." And he sang a line of a song: "*And sure what can't be cured, love, must be endured, love.*" He added: "The enduring is the curing." He was smiling, as usual.

The years passed. I stopped rearing animals for slaughter, and went in for market gardening instead. I got word of the lads occasionally. Clancy was teaching in Limerick and had a drink problem. Purcell was a journalist in the midlands and was married to a former Miss Ireland. Gallagher sent postcards from Alaska and Brazil; it wasn't clear what he was doing. Gavin had been ordained and was working with Irish emigrants in London.

I felt the sadness of the passing of time, and I was lonely for the want of a woman. I did nothing about it, I just hoped a woman would come to me. And it happened.

It was September 1976; I was 30 years of age. She knocked at my door one evening while I was having my tea. She was wearing a simple long grey dress, and there was a rucksack at her feet.

"I'm hungry." she said. "Could I join you at your meal?"

She ate in silence. I took her to be a couple of years younger than myself. She had lovely chestnut hair, and her skin was very white. Her lips were a little on the large side and her eyes were calm and kind of sad; they were the colour of the lichen on my apple-trees. I thought she was beautiful.

"I'm a travelling woman," she said eventually. "I'm not one of the travelling people, I'm just a travelling woman." She stood up, thanked me for the meal and headed out into the dusk. I never thought of offering her a bed.

She turned up again in the New Year. I told her there was a bed for her any time she wanted it. She thanked me, but left after her meal, which was as silent as the first one. She was back in the summer, and said she'd like to spend the night. I made up a bed in the room that young Malachy used to sleep in; it was my own until my father died. When I got up in the morning I saw her walking up from the lake, wrapped in a big green towel.

In the Autumn she stayed a week, and she went for her swim every morning. She helped me at the potato-digging and seemed to enjoy it. I loved her company, though she hardly ever said a word. You'd just hear a bit of humming out of her now and again. She disappeared after a week, saying nothing, and I didn't see her again till the following summer; that would have been 1978. She stayed three weeks and again we worked happily together in the garden. She came and went a few more times over the next year, and one evening – it was the evening the Pope was in Knock – I proposed to her. We were sitting at the table, eating brown bread and blackberry jam I'd made myself, and I said, "Will you marry me?"

"I'd never give you a child," says she.

"That wouldn't bother me," says I. "Will you be my wife anyway?"

"I'm a travelling woman," says she, "I'd be coming and going."

"I could live with that," says I, "I'd like you to be my woman anyway."

"All right," says she.

"Would it be any harm to ask you your name?" says I.

"Angela," says she, "Angela McGreal."

She went to her own bedroom that night, which sort of surprised me. And that's the way things stayed for her next few visits. Then one night I woke up to find her in my bed. I put my arms around her and for some reason these lines ran through my mind:

Home is the sailor, home from sea,
And the hunter home from the hill.

172

I put my hand on her breast and she said, "That's grand."

I moved my hand lower, but she placed it back on her breast and said, "That'll do grand."

I was a bit disappointed, of course, but it was still a great happiness to hold and be held by a woman. Every night after that she'd come to me after the light was out, and she'd be gone for her swim before I'd wake. I loved the closeness, and it did me good; I became a sunnier kind of person. I remember saying to Joe a thing I'd never have said before: "Joe," I said, "I think your complaint is all in the mind; maybe, deep down, you don't want to be cured."

He wasn't pleased.

Angela headed off again after Christmas and I didn't see her again until May. That became the pattern. I'd wake up some morning and find her gone; I'd come in some evening and there she'd be. She'd never tell me where she'd been, and I'd never ask. I took her as I found her; I blossomed in her company and I found great comfort in her body beside mine at night. None of the neighbours ever said a word about her comings and goings. And it never occurred to me to ask if they knew anything about her, any more than I asked herself.

More years passed. The gardening was going well and I was happy at it. I was down to the one cow now and I always milked her by the water tank, in memory of Malachy. Every now and again I'd hear something about the others. Gavin was teaching theology in an English seminary. Clancy had lost his teaching post and was working for a bookie; he was on the dry. Purcell was editor of a provincial paper now but Miss Ireland had left him. Gallagher sent postcards form Australia and Tibet. Whenever I dropped a line to any of them I made no mention of Angela.

I got to know her better over the years. She remained as quiet as ever, but her silences weren't always the same. I noticed her expressions, her gestures, her movements, I was aware of her different moods. On wet days she often sat by the kitchen window, staring at the rain, and rocking ever so slightly; a bomb could have gone off and she wouldn't have noticed. In the garden she could kneel for minutes studying some plant or insect; it would be pointless trying to catch her attention then. Sometimes, on a fine day, she would slip away from the garden and sit by the lake, and I'd hear her singing, in a gentle, plaintive voice; I never went near her and I couldn't make out the words: lullabies or laments they sounded like. I never made a comment to her after: I didn't want to kill her song. In bed sometimes she could be miles away, she'd be so still I'd wonder had I a dead woman in my arms.

Around Easter 1989 I heard that some man was renovating the old chapel. It hadn't been used since 1960 and was in a parlous state. The man turned out to be Father Lyons, our old woodwork teacher. He had been suspended from the priesthood, he told me. The old temper was the cause of it: he had struck the bishop in an argument and had refused to apologise. He had worked on the buildings in England for a few years and now he had the bishop's permission to restore the chapel for cultural purposes. Reparation was what he was at, he said, laughing, though he still had not apologised. I asked him if he had enjoyed being a priest. He had hated every minute of it, he said; he should never have been ordained.

"Why did you stay a priest, then?" I asked him.

"To punish myself," he said. "To punish myself . . . for being a bad priest."

He laughed again and, to tell the truth, I thought he wasn't the full shilling. I continued to drop in on him now and again just the same.

On Christmas morning1990 Angela gave me her first gift ever, the shell of a curlew's egg, and that night she said to me, "I want to be one flesh with you."

Those were her exact words: "I want to be one flesh with you."

The deed was done; it was the first time for both of us. We lay together afterwards for a long time, in silence.

"What are you thinking?" I asked her.

"This is my body," she answered. "This is my blood. I can hardly believe it."

We scarcely got out of bed all that week. On New Year's morning I asked Angela again what she was thinking.

"God made man in His image and likeness," says she. "Male and female He made them. God's likeness is male and female together, not apart. We're the image of God rightly, the two of us, this past week."

I'd never heard her make as long a speech. And for the first time ever, I saw her smile.

I was in great spirits at this stage, of course, and again I spoke strangely to Joe. His wife, Julia, was complaining of migraine, and I said to him, "Joe, sure maybe all she needs is a rub of the relic."

"I'm surprised at you," was all he said.

I called on Father Lyons shortly after and asked him about man being the image of God. He gave a dry laugh and said, "John Donne wrote that man is a sick God; I sometimes think God is a sick god."

And he gave a little cackle. When I got home that evening there was no sign of Angela.

Some time in March I had a card from Gallagher: he was in India but would be home in May, and would try to arrange a gang reunion at my place. Gavin wrote a few weeks later to say he couldn't make it: he had just been made an auxiliary bishop and was too busy. He was aware that I had found happiness with a woman and he sent me his blessing.

Gallagher and Purcell turned up on the appointed date: Clancy had gone on the batter and couldn't be traced. The three of us chatted for ages. When Purcell heard Father Lyons was above in the chapel he went quiet and soon headed for bed. I asked Gallagher to tell me about his travels.

"I won't tell you where I went," he said. "But I will tell you why. I was in search of wisdom, and in search of a woman. I never told you why I went to the seminary, did I? Well, one day just after my Leaving Cert, I was walking by the river outside the town when I heard screams from around the next turn. I ran, and saw a girl of about fifteen on the grass, naked, with two young fellows hunched over her. One of them skedaddled, and I beat the shite out of the other. The girl had been swimming and she was in such a state of shock that I had to help her to dry and dress. I managed to do that without really looking at her . . . I asked her where she lived and she said, 'The Orphanage.' That was half a mile away, and I walked with her, feeling shy for the first time in my life. I asked her a few more questions and she answered in a word or two each time. At the orphanage door she turned to me and said, 'Thank you. Thank you.' I'll never forget the expression on her face; I've never seen a face to match it since. Her hair was like a soft red-gold cloud, and she had grey-green eyes that had pain in them, and understanding, and pity, and the hint of a smile on her lips seemed like the hint of an infinite tenderness. I was looking at a beauty there are no words for. I know it sounds mad, but I thought I was looking at the face of God. I called back to ask for her two days later, and was told by a nun that she'd run away. To relatives? I asked. She had none, she'd been abandoned as a baby. What was her name? Angela. Angela what? Angela nothing; she had no name, she was Angela because she was sent by God. For weeks I thought about ways to look for her, but decided it was impossible. I was *certain* I would never see that expression again, that face that showed me God. And that's why I decided to be a priest: I would try to leap straight up the cliff instead of climbing the twisty path. I got disillusioned, of course; the intellectual fare was insipid. I decided to seek wisdom elsewhere. And in my search I've been seeking Angela too, looking for that look. I've known beautiful women, and loved some, but that first glimpse of God is imprinted on my soul and keeps me thirsting."

I said nothing.

Next day I had to row Joe out on to the lake: the mayfly was up. By teatime there were a dozen trout in the boat. Joe made a final cast, and hooked something heavy: it was a body, a naked body, face down.

"It's Angela," I said, and it was, all stiff and blue and bloated. We got her into the boat and then I stood up and shouted, "Fuck you, God! Fuck you, fuck you, fuck you!"

Then I collapsed sobbing on top of her. Joe lifted me up and put me in his seat; he covered Angela with an oilskin and took the oars. Through my tears I gazed at her feet among the trout while Joe rowed us home.

He carried her into his house and laid her on a bed. Julia plucked the weeds from her hair. I fell on my knees beside the bed and cried: "Angela, my Angela, my Angela."

I felt a hand on my head; it was Gallagher's. Joe led me to the kitchen. Purcell was there and he put his arm around me. When Gallagher came from the bedroom he whispered to Joe, "She was four months pregnant."

The post-mortem proved him right.

We buried her in our family plot, beside my parents. Joe and Julia and Gallagher and Purcell kept me going. And Father Lyons too. Her clothes were found a few miles up the lakeshore, and her green towel.

Purcell left the day of the funeral, but Gallagher stayed on; he had no plans. It dawned on me after a few days that something strange had happened to Joe: he had been cured in the boat, but they nearly had to carry him into the graveyard. I said it to Gallagher.

"I'll take a look at him," he said.

I sat in the kitchen with Julia while they went into a bedroom. They were ages there, and then we heard an unmerciful shout from Gallagher. They came out soon after, and Joe was as sprightly as a twenty-year-old.

"It's all in the mind," was all Gallagher would say later.

Joe said he'd hypnotized him and lunged at him with a knife. He's healthy ever since, but he never went out on the lake again.

I called to see Father Lyons. He said Purcell had dropped in on him before going home and told him he had hated him for 27 years.

"And how did you answer him?" I asked him.

"I asked him to hear my confession," says he. "He was stunned, of course, but I went down on my knees and made a general confession of my sins. And he forgave me, and we smiled at one another and embraced."

As I was leaving, Father Lyons put a hand on my shoulder and said, "I don't believe God is cruel. A father who sees his son die knows about suffering. And the dying son knows suffering. When God makes us suffer, His intention can't be bad. Maybe we *are* sick gods. And maybe suffering is the cure."

Gallagher stayed two years. He worked with me in the garden and he helped Father Lyons with the chapel. When that job was finished, Lyons went hunting for another church to repair, and Gallagher decided to move on.

"After all, I'm a travelling man," says he.

God knows where he's gone. I miss him. For two years he slept in Malachy's bed, we ate at the same table, and we dug and planted together in the garden. Without his company I might have followed Malachy's example. We didn't talk that much and we didn't talk that personally. I asked him once where he had got that pack of cards. It had belonged, he told me, to his great-grandfather, who had notions of being a novelist: he assigned a character to every card and an ambition to every character; that was as far as the novel ever got. When he died, the cards passed to his daughter who was a nun, and when she was old and blind she gave them to Gallagher, saying she'd used them for years as an aid to prayer when she couldn't keep her mind on anything else. With that history then, I asked him, was it not a great pity to send them floating down the river the way he did? They had served a serious purpose, he said, they had done their job. Besides, the pack was incomplete, since he knew we would all want to keep the cards we chose. And 'twas true for him as far as I was concerned: the two things I valued most in the house were the seven of spades and the shell of a curlew's egg.

Gallagher said next to nothing about his travels, and I told him just as little about my Angela. I often wondered if she was his Angela as well, and I'm sure he must have wondered that too, but somehow the subject never came up.

I was talking to an old acquaintance last night – Kate Butler, a former nun – and she said, 'Standing still is no guarantee that you'll get anywhere, but it's a necessary first step.' Does that shed any light on what you've read, Tessie, or is it a load of bull?

I can tell where some of the story came from: If I had a fiver for every young lad I've seen savaged by a priest, for example, I'd have a tenner. But mainly what I see here is the picture of a passive man, the image of myself. Let me explain.

Back in my early 30s, I suffered from all kinds of anxieties. I went from shrink to shrink, but no change came till one young lassie, having listened to me for an hour, said, 'Get real! Get a life!' and ended our meeting. It happened that that evening I had to attend, at the request of a sick aunt, the removal of an elderly Mrs Dale. When I got to the morgue, I learned that there were two corpses to be despatched, those of a Mrs Dale and a Mrs Doyle. Mentally I heard my father referring to my mother's favourite radio programme as 'Mrs Doyle's Dairy', and in confusion I entered the wrong room. The chief mourner was a dusky beauty who seemed hardly out of her teens; in the coffin was her mother, looking not much older and just as stunning. I stuck around, and as the rosary was struck up I heard two grinning, whispering men behind me refer to the daughter as 'Zoë', 'the gypsy', and 'the mare'.

As the coffin was hearsed, the young woman approached me and said, 'I'll see you at the graveyard tomorrow.' She did: I was under a spell. And after the burial she sought me out and said, 'You'll come back to the hotel for a meal.' I did. Crazy as it seems, the meal flowed into Zoë's twenty-first birthday party; it would have been too awkward to cancel. I floated around in a daze: ' Zoë' means 'Life', Tessie, and here was I being beckoned by life, drawn into life, getting a life, as the shrink had bid me. I was still dazed, though not amazed, when, some time the following morning, Zoë took me by the hand and led me upstairs to a bedroom, where I submitted, with whatever remnant of will I was left with, to the most delicious experience of my life. She was happy with me: 'my little toyboy' she kept calling me, or rather, 'me little tie-bye'. I was still not amazed when she announced around dawn: 'You'll marry me.' What did I say, Tessie? That's right, Tessie, that's what I said. I wasn't put off by what a cousin of Zoë's (female) said to me a few days later: 'Zoë was rode by ten men before she mounted you.' I was bothered less by the statistics than by the choice of verbs. We married anyway, and what I remember most keenly from the wedding is the embarrassment I was made to feel over my attempt at a joke during my speech. It concerned an African village where the women toiled unendingly, rearing children, gathering berries and grain, preparing and cooking food, while the men sat on their arses doing nothing, except once a fortnight when they went hunting and killed a pig. The punch-line was that a scientific study had shown that the fortnightly pig provided exactly the amount of protein the village needed. Twelve years and six children later, I'm not allowed to forget that 'joke': any time I've complained about the current pregnancy and the repercussions for the family

*finances, she has smiled menacingly and told me to 'get out there
and bring home more protein'. That's what explains my placename
lectures on radio, as well as up and down the country, to ICA
groups, Heritage Committees, Residents' Associations, Chambers
of Commerce and what not. She prefers me out of the house.
'Don't touch it, you'll make a balls of it!' she shouts, if I approach
a malfunctioning toaster or a dripping tap. She hardly lets me
pick up a child, I'd drop it. Yes, 'get out and bring home more
protein' . . . and I do, I do, to the point where I hate half the
placenames in the country, for the memories they provoke of
listening to myself droning on once again to a dozen people in a
draughty hall. But if I bring home protein, it's Zoë who does
everything else; would you believe, she survives on three hours
sleep a night? And if I've given the impression that she is totally
exasperated with me, that's not accurate; in one sphere I appear
to measure up. But that's another story.*

*Apart from that, I can make sense of a few more details: I had
notions of taking up fishing one time, but I'm too busy; I'd never
send a child to a boarding-school, and Zoë favours green towels.*

All the best, Tessie,

Love,

Enda Ring.

WAITER

Dear Monsieur Beckett,

I've been told you were approachable, so I'm approaching you.

You loom large in my mind. Having read that yours is the kind of intellect that appears only once every 500 years, I am angry at being unable to see that. Two or three of your books have made me laugh more than all others combined; they are written, besides, in a style both exquisite and simple. As for your bleakness, nay, your horror of existence, it is doubtless superbly evoked, but I find it in itself unremarkable.

You have had, it may interest you to hear, a crucial role in my love-life, such as it has been. I was paying court to a younger student, Agatha Payne, whose attractions I cannot recall. She was religious, and of a nervous disposition – the kind of young lady on whose exam desk an ID card will be flanked by at least two of the following: crucifix, miraculous medal, prayer to St Jude, bottle of Lourdes water, Padre Pio relic, scapulars.

A student of French and Philosophy, she attended a study circle organised by a Marxist group, and found her faith under serious attack. She sought reassurance from me, who was not well placed to give it, my own faith having decamped some time

185

before. (A fact of which I neglected to inform her.) I suggested that she abandon the study circles, but the more they troubled her, the more she felt compelled to attend.

We studied side by side, and I noticed a new habit: at the top of each page of notes she wrote SBSGB. I was familiar, of course, with SAG and SWALK, and even with AMDG, but what was this SBSGB? It was inspired, she told me, by a detail in some Irish writer's newspaper account of a visit to you in Paris: 'Samuel Beckett says God Bless.' 'It means Beckett believes in God, Enda; I think that's hugely important, don't you?' And she launched into an exposition of the Christian meaning of Godot: the fruitfulness of the Cross and all that. Looking into her large liquid eyes, I found her at that moment excruciatingly desirable. I suggested that we meet in her place that evening for a discussion of your work.

My plan was simple: to make her forget the comforts of religion and learn the consolations of sex. It didn't work out; I flopped spectacularly. Agatha became hysterical and threw me out, and she never spoke to me again. Someone told me she had tried to enter a posh convent at Easter, but was turned down because she had been born out of wedlock. She failed her exams, summer and autumn, and left college; I don't know where her nerves took her after that.

I won't bother you with the details of where mine have taken me. I'd appreciate it, though, if you cast your eye on a story; it's about imprisonment and inarticulacy, about which I know a little and I know you know a lot.

I spent my first seventeen years in an orphanage in Limerick. And till the age of seven I had an inseparable friend. We were known as the twins, though we had the same first name, Isabelle; she was Hand, I was Hehir; she was dark, I was fair. The Sunday after our First Communion, Mother Pelagia put the two of us in a car and drove us to a house outside the city. There we had a meal with some children and some grown-ups, and I asked a girl if the food was cooked by a nun or a maid.

"No," she said, "Mammy does all that," and then I made everyone laugh – everyone except Isabelle – by asking, "What's a mammy?"

The next Sunday we were sailing paper boats in a gutter behind the chapel when Mother Pelagia appeared, carrying a bag, and told Isabelle to go with her. I followed, and watched Isabelle and the bag being put in a car. Then the car moved off, and it was driven by the Mammy. I ran after it, calling Isabelle, but Mother Pelagia caught me and told me I was a twin no longer; Isabelle was going to live in the house we'd been in last Sunday. I went hysterical, of course, and cried for God knows how long, but what I remember most clearly from the rest of that day is the efforts of one of the kitchen-maids to distract me; she had a limp and we called her Hopalong, but her name was really Sally. She began by doing tricks with matches, but I had no interest; anyway, matches were outside my experience. She went away for a while and came back with a banana; when we peeled it, the eaty bit fell out in a dozen pieces, like so many fat fruity Communions. I didn't appreciate the magic, though it was my first banana, and her explanations about needle and thread confused me. Then she really mesmerized me, with a yard of thick twine. She stretched it out, looped it and cut it in half; then she cupped her hands around it and stretched it out again; it was all there again in one piece! I felt a thrill run through me, I actually wet myself a bit. She did it again, and again and again and again. Then she showed me how it was done, and tried to teach me. I went through a mile of twine, but I found the trick unlearnable; I was convinced that Sally had real magic.

She was my special friend after that, although we met only once or twice a week. And nobody minded, even though she was a grown-up, even older than most of the nuns. She was from Rosmuc in Connemara, and she began to teach me songs in Irish. The first one, I remember, was 'Bean Pháidín', about a woman who wanted another woman's husband. Then she taught me 'Cailleach an Airgid' and 'Faoitín' and 'Peigín Leitir Móir'. And as I grew older the songs got better: over the ten years of our friendship I learned 'Róisín Dubh', 'Úna Bhán', 'An Gabha Ceartan', 'An Sceilpín Draighneach', and a few dozen more great songs of love and lament; I jumped through the hoops of umpteen exams, but my real education came from Sally.

After I left the orphanage, I moved to Galway to study nursing. And during my second year there, I entered for a singing competition at the Oireachtas in Carraroe. It was there I first laid eyes on the most beautiful young man I'd ever seen. He was sitting in a pub between two girls and singing 'Casadh an tSugáin', and his yellow hair, blue eyes and mischievous grin gave him the look of an angel off duty. What made him extra sexy was a little gold ring winking in his ear. I was told he was a Christy Looney from Killnaboy. I didn't care what crazy name he had, I was smitten. I caught his eye a couple of times and got a wink and a smile. I saw him again later, outside the hall where I was to sing: he was being hassled by an unpleasant-looking older bloke. When I was a few feet away, the older bloke threw a punch at him and turned away. Christy's earring went flying and a trickle of blood flowed down his neck. I whipped off my scarf and applied it to the wound; he took it, thanked me, said he was all right and walked off in a daze. I went and sang my song – 'Tá na páipéir dhá saighneáil', because it had a verse about an orphan girl who didn't want any man to ruin her. I came nowhere; the *moltóir* said I had one of the finest voices he had ever heard, but he criticized my pronunciation of Irish. I swore I would never again sing a song in that language. I went looking for Christy afterwards but failed to find him. And during the rest of my time in Galway I never came across him again. Remembering him, I found every other man woefully wanting.

I went to Dublin in 1985, to work in Vincent's. Early the following January I looked after a patient who was admitted with suspected food poisoning; Mark Grogan his name was, – a fine-looking man of 42 with piercing green eyes and fair hair. The doctors were baffled: tests failed to establish the presence of the expected bacteria, and the patient was not responding to treatment. Then he told me what he had not told the doctors: that he'd got sick within minutes of learning that the 'turkey' he'd eaten in a salad a week earlier was goose. Within an hour of telling me, he was as right as rain. He took me out to dinner on my next free evening.

"I have no past," he said, after getting me to talk for an hour about the orphanage. His present was alluded to, casually and piecemeal, then and on later occasions. He mentioned investments, property dealings. There was a racehorse or two down the country, a pub somewhere, he had the finest yacht in Howth. He would say 'my accountant' and 'my solicitor'. He had a Porsche as well as the BMW. He divided his nights between an apartment in Malahide and the family home in Laytown. On Shrove Tuesday he asked me to marry him. I said yes. In the early hours of Ash Wednesday I gave him my virginity in Malahide. (When I asked him if he wanted to take precautions, he laughed and said he always did that; he'd given more false names than he could remember. Then, more seriously, he added that he'd had a vasectomy years before.)

The wedding, in June, was to be tiny – just ourselves and the witnesses; the priest was someone he'd been to school with, the church was in a little country place outside Trim. Three days before the date, one of my nursing classmates was drowned on a visit home to Westport. I travelled down by train for the funeral; Mark was to collect me afterwards and drive me back to Laytown. But it wasn't Mark who turned up at the cemetery, it was Christy Looney. He didn't recognize me and I was too shocked to say a word. Mark couldn't make it, he explained; *he* was a cousin of Mark's and worked for him every summer. (He was a woodwork teacher based in Sligo.)

Of our first hour's conversation I remember no topics, only Christy's voice and laughter. Somewhere in Roscommon he said he'd packed a picnic basket, and he turned into a bog road. He brandished a bottle of wine (red), then discovered that one of his two glasses was cracked. We'd have to share, he said, and he filled the good glass and handed it to me with a bow and a smile. I took a sip, and gave it back to him. It passed between us a few more times. After my third sip, there was only a little wine left – just enough to cover Christy's ear-ring which was my treasure since Carraroe. He drained the glass and froze. He tried to speak, but couldn't. We looked at each other for an age, then our heads came together in slow motion. His face went out of focus and was all the more beautiful, and I felt him kiss my cheeks and then my chin; then his lips were on mine and it was the moment I had dreamed about for half of seven years. The picnic had to wait – a long time; as Christy put it, the grace before was more important than the meal – and we polished it off as we drove. Swapping information about ourselves took us most of the way. He had always called Mark his uncle, he explained, although he was in fact his first cousin once removed; as it happened, people often said he was like him. As we headed out of Navan, I grabbed his arm and said, "Let's not go to Mark; let's go away somewhere together and be happy."

He said, "You don't know Mark Grogan. If we tried anything he'd have me skinned alive, and you'd wish you weren't a woman; there's no place we could hide from him. But I'll be seeing you; aren't there lots of jobs to be done in your house over the next two months?"

The wedding went ahead as planned. (Sally sent us a card, however she knew about us.) For the honeymoon, Mark had organised a bird-watching tour of the west coast. His enthusiasm showed me a new side to him, but despite the magnificent binoculars he gave me, I took little interest at first; in Donegal and Sligo I spent much of my time gazing lazily at the scenery or mulling over the new words drifting into my vocabulary: whimbrel, kittiwake, chiffchaff, shoveler, wheatear, whinchat, siskin, twite, bartailed godwit, little stint . . . Those last two especially sent me into reveries. But my mind was wonderfully concentrated by an incident on the north Mayo coast. We had just got out of the car to do a cliff walk when I heard Mark crying out, "Jesus Christ! That fucker shouldn't be here!" with as much fear as anger in his voice. His binoculars were trained on a large bird quite a distance away and heading towards us; seconds later he was taking a shotgun from the boot of the car; he fired, and the bird crashed onto the rocks 50 feet from us.

"Go you," he said, "and dump that bastard over the cliff."

I did, with my gorge rising at the sight of the blood-spattered feathers and the touch of the jerking legs.

"What was it?" I asked him.

"A greylag goose," he answered, "and we're heading further south, where there's less chance of them."

We got into the car and he drove non-stop to Clifden. For the rest of the trip I was all attention, but I needed no binoculars for the watching I was doing.

Back in Laytown, I was immediately in tension. Christy was working on Mark's yacht in Howth, and I didn't know when he'd be coming to work in the house. When he turned up one evening with Mark, I couldn't look either of them in the eye. When Mark asked me to prepare a bed in the guest room, I blushed. Next morning he gave Christy his instructions and told me I was going with him to Dublin: he had me booked in for a two-hour driving lesson. When the three of us sat down to our dinner that evening, Mark was the only one who could talk; Christy and I could barely answer his occasional questions. There were two more days like that, and then Mark told me my next driving lesson was cancelled. When he drove off next morning on his own, I was a bundle of nerves. I didn't dare to approach Christy, I stayed at the other end of the house. Mark popped in about mid-day, but only for a minute, to pick up something, and spoke to neither of us. At dinner, I couldn't eat, and I went to bed early with a headache. An hour later the bedroom door opened, the light was switched on, and Mark ushered Christy in.

"OK, Christy," he said. "Strip. Go ahead, Isabelle is stripped already, as near as dammit; ye can have the ride, I see ye're both dying for it for days. Have yeer ride then, don't mind me. Go on, man, what's keeping you?"

Christy left the room. Mark got into bed beside me without a word. Next morning his car roared down the avenue before 8:00. I leapt out of bed and ran from the room. On the landing I crashed into Christy, who was making the same journey in reverse. We decided on my room, and if Mark had returned in the next hour to shoot us, we wouldn't have heard him coming, and we'd have died happy.

He didn't catch us that morning, of course, but he did catch us in the middle of the day a fortnight later. And he didn't shoot us, of course, he just told us to get the hell out of his sight and never to reappear. We couldn't believe our luck. We stopped the car a few times to kiss and laugh, and once when we kissed I cried and cried and cried. Christy had an idea; he phoned a friend in Athlone and arranged to borrow a little cruiser; we took it up the Shannon and honeymooned for a fortnight. Everything was pleasure: cooking, eating, cleaning, cruising, swimming, lovemaking, talking, drinking in riverside pubs, shopping in sleepy villages, walking in lush countryside. We didn't care whether it rained or shone, both our watches stopped, we hardly knew night from day.

Christy told me things about Mark. He was an only child, and when he was seven, his father hanged himself in prison, where he was starting a sentence for embezzlement. His mother never again left the house until she died of shame six years later. Mark then went to live with his mother's brother and his wife, Christy's grandparents, in Spanish Point. Christy was only a toddler when Mark returned, at 21, to live in Laytown. His ambition, he had told Christy, was to be the strongest man in Ireland. ("For strong, read ruthless.") His real name, by the way, wasn't Grogan: that was just what the locals called him in West Clare, and what he later adopted by deed-poll; his real name was Graugans; his grandfather had come from Germany after the First World War.

In Leitrim village one evening, beside the ruins of a castle of the O'Rourkes, we read an inscription marking the spot where

Brian Óg O'Rourke welcomed Donal O'Sullivan Beare after his fourteen-day march from West Cork in January, 1602; of his thousand followers, only 35 had survived, and only one was a woman, the wife of O'Sullivan's uncle Diarmuid. Christy kissed me with a fierceness he'd never shown before.

"My uncle's wife, oh, my uncle's wife," he breathed into my ear. "Let's go back to the boat."

We were lost in a kiss when we were set upon. Mark's arms pinioned mine and Christy was seized by two heavies. I watched them beat him unconscious, then I was bundled into a car. The three men discussed the Galway races from which they were evidently returning; a horse owned by Mark had come second.

Back in Laytown, Mark explained the new regime. My room would be the one on the top floor which had always been locked before; I would not interfere with its décor or present contents. I would be available to sleep with him in the master bedroom whenever he summoned me, and I would not be there in the morning when he awoke. When he intended bringing home another woman, he would phone me, and I would make myself scarce. I would not make any phone-calls, write letters, or open the letterbox. I would not enter any shop in the village or anywhere else; a weekly delivery of groceries would arrive from Drogheda. I would have his dinner ready each evening at 7:30; I would eat separately. I could take a daily walk between 12:00 and 1:00, on the strand or on country roads, but I would not engage in conversation with anyone. I would keep the house spick and span, and the garden free of weeds. The rest of my time I could spend as I pleased, but in the house I would find neither television nor radio, neither books nor newspapers.

My room was the one Mark had slept in as a child. On the walls were pictures of birds and newspaper photographs of horses, including a series of four showing the Queen Mother's horse, Devon Loch, slithering along the ground and losing the Grand National to ESB. There was a wardrobe full of a boy's clothes all in perfect condition, from a seven-year-old's sailor suit to a teenager's riding gear. A large window with several small panes provided a view of the beach and the sea.

I followed the regime to the letter, except that I never took walks. The house gleamed, I terrorized the weeds, I cooked good meals. Two or three nights a week, I felt Mark's weight upon me; as soon as he slept I escaped to the shower. Some nights – even two or three nights in a row – he would not come home; he never let me know in advance. There were phone-calls telling me to make myself scarce. I gave them names: Tara, Clara, Laoise, Nina, Emily, but perhaps it was the same one all the time. To stop thinking about Christy, I tried telling myself he was dead. Cleaning a mirror in October, I thought I saw the eye of a madwoman.

One day I ventured into the attic. I found a book, an old missal, inscribed: *In the name of God and of the dead generations, Josie Looney, Coláiste Mhuire, 2/2/22.* Underneath that was written: *Up God! Patsy Minogue, 13/2/22.* And *Up the rebels! Sylvie O'Dea, 1/7/22.*

It became the secret pantry of my mind.

I nibbled at the proper of the Mass, the appurtenances of the chalice, the celebrant's vestments; I savoured the lives of the saints . . . St Thomas Aquinas joined the Dominicans at nineteen; his brothers kidnapped him and locked him up for a year, but he didn't change his mind. He died in 1274 on his way to the Ecumenical Council at Lyons. Pope Leo XIII declared him Patron of all Catholic schools. St Remigius was appointed Bishop of Rheims in France at the extraordinary age of 22, and reigned until his 97th year. He baptized Clovis, king of the Franks. Four of his letters have survived, as well as verses written to be engraved on a chalice. St Petronilla was long venerated as the daughter of St Peter; recent study has shown however that she belonged to the Roman family of the Aurelii. St Zephyrinus, a third-century pope, outlawed wooden chalices in the celebration of Mass. St Bonaventure taught in Paris at the same time as St

Thomas Aquinas. In 1265 he declined the archbishopric of York, but eight years later was created Cardinal Bishop of Albano by Pope Gregory X. When his Cardinal's hat was brought to him he told the legates to hang it on a nearby tree as he was washing dishes and his hands were wet and greasy. He died the following year while playing a prominent role in the Ecumenical Council at Lyons. The Pope and the entire Council took part in his funeral; every priest in the world said Mass for his soul. His emblem is a cardinal's hat.

And I wolfed down the Thanksgiving after Communion, prayers by Sts Thomas Aquinas and Bonaventure; St Aquaventure I called them.

And do thou, O heavenly Father, vouchsafe one day to call me, a sinner, to the ineffable banquet where thou, together with Thy Son and the Holy Ghost, art to Thy saints true and unfailing light, fulness of content, joy for evermore, gladness without alloy, consummate and everlasting happiness . . . Grant that my soul may hunger for Thee, who art the bread of angels, the comforting nourishment of all holy souls, our daily and most delectable bread, our supersubstantial bread, in which is found every sweet delight. May my heart ever hunger for Thee, on whom the angels lovingly gaze; may it feed on Thee; and may the innermost depths of my being be filled with the sweetness which comes from having tasted Thee. May my soul ever thirst for Thee, Who art the source of life, the fount of wisdom and knowledge, the brightness of everlasting light, the flood of all true happiness, the riches of the house of God.

It was Christy I hungered and thirsted for. I prayed with intensity and without hope. Time passed, and I watched my life happen at a distance, like a film about somebody else. Sometimes I laughed a little for no reason, or sang bits of skipping-songs. I played he-loves-me-he-loves-me-not with a comb. Flowers whose names I didn't know I called maniples, chasubles, dalmatics, graduals, patens; weeds were shearwaters, greenshanks, turnstones, phalaropes, smews, scaups.

One morning Christy drove up to the door. I panicked, but he laughed.

"Cheltenham," he said. "He never misses it, he'll be gone for the week."

He wanted me to come away with him on the spot; he might as well have asked me to fly, I couldn't imagine beyond the front gate. In my room he questioned me, and told me that I had to leave Mark. He was building a boat, like a small Galway hooker, we could sail anywhere in the summer, it would have the loveliest tumble-home you could imagine. When I didn't ask what that was, he put his hands on my waist and said my tumble-home was the most beautiful of all. I let him draw me down onto the bed, but for ages all I wanted to do was to lie there beside him in silence. Then at some point I imagined him gone, and I tore off my clothes in a panic. Over the next three days and nights we made love a dozen times. He said he'd return during the Galway races. When he left, I stared at the grey sea for several hours. Mark and normality returned. A fortnight later I knew that I hadn't conceived.

I found another book. A booklet really, wedged between a rafter and the roof of the old stable: *A Garland of Old Ballads*. It was shocking: the songs lit up my world with lurid lanterns; they were about adulteries, imprisonments, escapes, pursuits, murders . . . The first one I went back to was 'Little Musgrave and Lady Barnard'; it was about *us*, a man finding his wife in bed with another man:

> *The first stroke that Little Musgrave struck,*
> *It hurt Lord Barnard sore;*
> *The next stroke that Lord Barnard struck,*
> *Little Musgrave ne'er struck more. . . .*

He cut her paps from off her breast;
Great pity 'twas to see
That some drops of this lady's heart's blood
Ran trickling down her knee.

In no time I had the whole thing, and I chanted it over and over. And then I began to *hear* it, hear it sung, I mean, in my head. The tune I had never heard before; it was simple, but it was the perfect tune, the ideal fit for the words. I began to sing aloud, gingerly, and was astonished by what came out. As I grew accustomed to myself I sang with spirit, with a joy I hadn't known since our Shannon cruise. And in the weeks that followed, I sang it for myself hundreds of times, I was in no hurry to learn another song. I made it second nature; it could not have been better sung. The tragedy of the three didn't matter: out of their blood had come beauty. My daily tasks were a mere backdrop to the perfection in which I lived and moved. St Aquaventure suffered a serious eclipse.

One evening in June I stood at my window and watched horses racing on Laytown beach. I supposed Mark might have a mount there. In an early race a white horse led the field, a riderless shining white mare – I felt sure it was a mare; with my binoculars I could see her frothing at the mouth. As she drew level with me, she wheeled away to the left; I fancied she was returning to the sea from which she had surely come. She disappeared, and my eye caught a speck on the horizon. The races continued and the speck grew into sails, three red sails on a black hull. She remained too distant to be distinct; she just hovered offshore like a promise, maybe watching the races like me. Except that I wasn't watching the races, I was watching her, with a . . . with a kind of a spring in my heartbeat. As I was raising the window-sash, I noticed for the first time something scratched on a pane: the words *Anser anser anser*, each word savaged by an X, and a date, 23/2/56, which was the day Mark's mother died.

I moved on to another song: *Young Lord Bacon:*

> *Oh when she saw him, the Young Lord Bacon,*
> *The sight she could not bear,*
> *For the sleeky mice and the hungry rats*
> *Had eaten his yellow hair.*

> *She's given him a shaver for his beard,*
> *A new comb for his hair,*
> *And five hundred pounds to fill his pocket,*
> *To spend and not to spare . . . .*

> *And when she came to Lord Bacon's gate,*
> *She heard the music play;*
> *And well she knew from all she heard,*
> *It was his wedding day.*

> *'Oh tell him to send me some wedding-cake,*
> *And some wine both red and strong,*
> *And to remember well that lady fair,*
> *Who loosed his prison bonds.'*

Again I listened inside myself, and the air came, never before heard. Singing it, I lost awareness of my surroundings: on one occasion I found myself at the front gate, my hands gripping the bars; the noise of a truck sent me scurrying back to the house. Often I sang it at my window, gazing out on the sea.

Christy didn't show up at the time of the Galway races. For nine days I could not sing. And when I did find my voice, I turned to the song I had shied away from, finding it the saddest of all – 'Fair Annie of Loch Ryan':

> *'Take down, take down the mast of gold,*
> *Set up the mast of tree;*
> *It ill becomes a jilted dame*
> *To sail so gallantly.*

Take down, take down the sails of silk,
Set up the sails of skin;
The outside should not be so gay
When there's such grief within' . . . .

He catched her by the yellow hair,
And drew her to the strand;
But cold and stiff was every limb
Before he reached the land.

And first he kissed her cheek, her cheek,
And then he kissed her chin,
And then he kissed her ruby lips,
But there was no breath within.

Once I had it, it was as if I knew no other song. I sang it all the time, I lived it, I felt I would never sing anything else. I thought about death; my dreams were full of drownings.

One afternoon in September a beggar-woman came to the door. A heavy-set woman of 40 with amazingly white teeth and her dark hair in a bun. She stood some seconds without speaking, with the ghost of a smile, sizing me up.

"You'd do well to go to Connemara," she said, "to a place near the village of Carna, where the old people live."

I begged her pardon, and she repeated: "That's what I'm telling you now; you may go to Carna, to where the old people live."

I thanked her and proceeded to shut the door; she said, "You can thank me by giving me a few bits of old kids' clothes."

I had no children, I told her.

"Aye," she said, "just a few bits of old clothes."

What sent me to my room, I think, was less what she said than the yard of thick twine her fingers fiddled with all the time that she spoke. I returned with Mark's little sailor suit and his dandy riding outfit. She took one in each hand and said: "God give you good road, daughter."

I watched her walk away, the blue and white swinging gently in one hand, the red and white in the other. She had gone about 30 yards when the BMW roared around the bend of the avenue. She didn't step aside, she just stopped, and Mark braked. It was several seconds before he emerged from the car, then they looked at each other in silence for several more. Mark said a few words I didn't catch. Her reply was longer but no more distinct; she gestured in my direction. He got back in the car, did a U-turn on the lawn and sped away; the woman calmly continued her journey down the avenue.

An hour later Mark shot himself in his bedroom in Malahide. The woman was never traced.

Christy came for Mark's funeral, of course. 'Things cropped up' was his only excuse about the Galway races, things to do with his boat. I told him what the woman had said about the old people in Carna; he looked taken aback but said it was just nonsense and not worth telling the gardaí. We spent just one night together; we didn't make love. When I broached the subject of our future, he said we would talk another time, when the dust had settled; what I needed now above all was to grow gradually re-accustomed to normality.

For weeks and weeks I had dealings with legal people. That got me out, but there was as much unreality about streets and shops as there was about my new-found wealth. Even a walk on a country road could produce little frights.

I took driving lessons, and in early December I drove my Fiesta to Carna. There was an old people's home on the island of Muighinis, I was told. I found it. Between the ringing of the bell and the opening of the door I heard my opening line in my head:

"My name is Isabelle Hehir, I'm a nurse and I'd like to learn about running an old people's home."

I didn't get past my name, because of the look in my listener's eye.

"Come in," she said. "Come in, I'm your twin, I'm Isabelle Hand."

She boasted about her charges like a mother. Máire Pheadair had been a midwife for 40 years and had a nephew a TD; the radio crowd had been in to interview her a few days before. Cóilin Mór had been one of the finest storytellers around and had given stuff to Seamus Ennis; he had Alzheimer's now. Josie Dharach used to own three pubs in Boston and was well in with the Kennedys. Bríd Mhichael was 92 and nearly blind; she was always smiling, she was a saint. Father Willie's wits had been driven astray by brooding on the sins of the world. He spent all his time saying Mass; thirteen in one day was his record. The Archbishop had said to let him at it, he was harmless, but to make sure his wine-bottles contained grapejuice. Patsy Luke had done time in several prisons here and in England; in his day he was one of the few boxers who could give Máirtín Thornton a run for his money. Pádraic Jimmy had featured in at least two stories by Máirtín Ó Cadhain; a student from Sweden was recording his reminiscences. Her roll-call was interrupted by a woman who limped towards us; it took me a few seconds to recognize Sally. She grasped my two hands.

"Ah, Mother Pelagia,." she said. "You were always a mother to me."

I didn't notice that Isabelle was pregnant; she had to tell me she was six months gone. The father was a Clareman who lived in Sligo; he had come to Muighinis in June to study with the local boat-builders. When I could speak, I said, "Christy Looney is the great love of my life; just recently we have been discussing marriage."

I left.

Christy showed up within the week. Isabelle had torn strips off him, and didn't want to see him again. I told him I didn't either. It was the biggest shock of his life; he wept like a beaten schoolboy. He had turned to Isabelle out of loneliness, he said, and because she had reminded him of me; he had stood by her on account of the baby, but now that she had dismissed him we could marry as soon as it was decent. I produced a bottle of champagne. I had bought it for our engagement, I explained, but he could use it instead on his own to launch his boat. I have never seen such hurt as his face showed at that moment. He took the bottle. I expected him to come back to me in the next few weeks, but he never did.

I turned the house into a small convalescent home. Planning permission, legal requirements, Health Board regulations, structural alterations, dealings with builders and banks, hiring staff, all kept me busy. When Christy wrote to tell me of the birth of his son Diarmuid, I didn't reply. When he wrote a year later that he had moved to Muighinis and married Isabelle, I sent a card; my heart was bleeding, but I was installing my first six patients and I got on with it. When I heard on the radio four years later that Isabelle had died in a hit-and-run accident in Carraroe, I drove immediately to Muighinis.

The body had been brought home from the hospital. Christy sat by the coffin, white and stunned; I wasn't sure he noticed when I embraced him. But he noticed when Sally came limping over to me and said, "Ah, the two Isabelles, Isabelle and Isabelle, the twins. And, you know, yeer two mothers was sisters. That's right, but Mother Pelagia would never let me tell you. And I wouldn't mind only I knew your mother; didn't I comfort the poor girleen the day she left you in to the nuns? And I think I seen her since then too."

The thought flashed through my mind that my mother was the beggarwoman, and that she had let Mark know he was my father; but the idea was too outrageous and I dismissed it.

Nine months of enquiries on Christy's part proved Sally right about the sisters, though no further sane word came from her. Isabelle's mother was a Teresa Harte, who had died without identifying the father; my mother was her sister Monica. Christy was delighted with the link; he actually came to Laytown to show me the documentation. He was amazed that I wasn't dying to find my parents; his own obsession had made him neglect his boat, which was standing completed and half-tarred since Isabelle's death. This was our first meeting since the funeral; he was quieter than he used to be, as if he found me somehow intimidating.

I had just got back from Cleltenham the following March – a horse I had a share in was running there – when I heard the news that Christy was missing. His boat was found drifting on Cill Chiaráin Bay with nothing on board but the neck of a champagne bottle. Ten days later he was washed up at Leitir Caladh.

It took nearly a year, but I got custody of Diarmuid; Christy having no close relations and my mother not being traceable, I was deemed next of kin, as his first cousin once removed. He arrived last March, on his seventh birthday, in floods of tears; cake and candles did nothing for him, but I tried out Sally's banana trick and it cheered him up.

I put him in the room Mark put me in. A day or two later he came running to me with a book he had found under a floorboard: *A Bird-Book for the Pocket*, inscribed: '*To my darling Mark, on your tenth birthday, with all my love, Mummy, March 5th, 1953.*'

I flicked through it and found a single sentence underlined; it was on the page about the greylag goose: '*In danger, gander flies away leaving family.*'

The same page informed me that the Latin name of the bird was *Anser anser anser*.

Last month I had a visit from a German student; she was doing research on her great granduncle, Helmut Graugans, who had come to Ireland in 1918, and she had been directed to my address. At one point in our talk she said, "Graugans means grey goose."

I had a flash of insight and I said, "And not just any old grey goose either."

I enlightened her about the lag bit, but I scarcely heard myself speaking; I was watching a kaleidoscope of goose and geese, guns and ganders and dangers, hanging fathers and angry sons, Latin names and name-changes, all whirling into a picture that finally made some sense. Well, you learn something everyday.

Most days I just learn more about the same thing: what a mammy is.

I am the seven-year-old coming running with the book. An orphan, bubbling with life, joy, hope, he has no idea that further sufferings await him, or that his new mother will furnish him with most, like family heirlooms fatefully passed on. Hatred of one's parents is a basic mark of intelligence.

The shooting of the goose: when I was ten I blew the head off a stuffed snipe with my father's shotgun and made smithereens of its glass case. It was the only time the fucker ever beat me – angry with himself for having left the gun loaded.

Song: I'm glad it makes itself heard. It lets us rise for a few moments off the surface of the planet – cette putain de terre, as one of your characters calls it. I sing sometimes.

Isabelle calls things by wrong names. There are times when I have no names, no words; I am looking at things just made, unnamed, untamed. Other times, memory will pray, something flowery even, like Bonaventure. It doesn't bother me: prayer is noble, as worthy of respect as any way of facing the dazzling dark.

The nursing-home: was I thinking of my parents? Yes: they were never in one, but I was taking pleasure in imagining them lumped in there among other arthritics and Alzheimer's victims. In fact they were nursed at home, and I kept an eye on them at night. Every time my mother annoyed me, I would lead my father into her room and plonk him beside her bed. To witness his attempts at civility or aggression, and the distaste or terror in her eyes, was a source of great pleasure to me. When he misbehaved, I would ask him: 'Do you see this?', brandishing a small hatchet; he would skulk to his bed.

This regime ended with my father's death. He drank paraquat; he lasted a week. No one ever suggested that it was anything other than accidental. The coroner was lavish in his expression of sympathy, in view of my double bereavement: pushing my mother's wheelchair away from my father's grave, in blinding sunlight, in full view of 50 mourners, I stumbled at the top of a flight of steps, ejecting my surviving parent and propelling her with considerable force towards the bottom; she lasted a week.

One bit of pure wish-fulfilment on my part: the villain is cured of his psychosomatic food-poisoning by talking about it to his nurse. Would that all ills could be as easily disposed of. One happy consequence of my being orphaned was the cessation of the ritual of administering my parents' medication: the house had become a bloody pharmacy. And now the whirligig of time has brought back the bottles and the blisters, the droppers and the sachets and the tubes. Nightly I minister to myself for mania, depression, thick blood, high blood pressure, raised cholesterol, gout and a pile. I take, in addition, the occasional laxative, diuretic, antibiotic or supplementary painkiller. Among the risks to which I thus expose myself in the name of health and wellbeing are: pins and needles, tingling of the limbs, poor circulation, cold hands and feet, hand tremors, spasm in the fingers, smelly feet, headaches, dizziness, lightheadedness, tinnitus, blurred vision, double vision, yellowing of the whites of the eyes, yellowing of the skin, reddening of the skin, blistering of the skin, peeling of the skin, bruising, psoriasis, acne, rashes, runny nose, stuffy nose, swollen sinuses, swelling of the eyelids, swelling of the face, swelling of the tongue, swelling of the throat, swelling of the lips, difficulty in walking, difficulty in speaking, loss of memory, loss of pain sensation, loss of appetite, loss of weight, loss of hair, baldness, blindness, deafness, lockjaw, impaired consciousness, lack of co-ordination, muscle weakness, muscle cramps, muscle pain, muscle shaking, muscle twitching, inflamed blood vessels, high white blood cell count, low white blood cell count, anaemia, fainting, high temperature, fever, increased sweating, hot flushes, inflamed pancreas, overactive thyroid, underactive thyroid, goitre, frequent urination, kidney stones, kidney failure, inflammation of the liver, abnormal liver function, jaundice, hepatitis, gastritis, abdominal discomfort, stomach ulcers, leg ulcers, mouth ulcers, gum swelling, tooth decay, dry mouth, dry cough, dry skin, dry eyes, asthma, shortness of breath, wheezing, sneezing, burping, farting, taste disorder, prolonged thirst, indigestion, nausea, vomiting, blood in the vomit, constipation, diarrhoea, hard stools, soft stools, black stools, back pain, joint pain, palpitations, uneven heart rate, chest pain, disease of the heart muscle, heart attack, stroke, intestinal perforations, total body itch, insomnia, yawning, tiredness, lethargy, disturbed sleep, nightmares, nervousness, restlessness, mood changes, agitation, confusion, disorientation, anxiety, fits, psychoses, hallucinations, delirium, sexual disturbances, erectile dysfunction, abdominal cramps, male breast enlargement, aching nipples, inflamed gullet, anaphylactic shock, loosening of the fingernails, loosening of the toenails, mania, depression, thick blood, high blood pressure, raised cholesterol, gout, death and piles. No doubt there are more: some products come without a warning, but their innocence is not to be presumed.

My list of ailments will have awakened unpleasant memories for you. With no ill-effect, I trust. Sincerely, thank you for your time.

Yours diffidently,

Enda Ring.

DAME

Dear Dame Julian,

You have been the fitful beacon that replaced my faith. A sentence you wrote is the most consoling utterance in history.

I was in second year in college when a classmate, Patricia ('Paddy') Kinsella, began to pester me. First it was blushes and smiles, then she was sitting next to me at lectures, issuing supposed witticisms for my amusement. With her acne and thick glasses, I found her unattractive. One day she presented me with a stack of pages photocopied from reference books on Shakespeare; when I said I'd return them soon she said, 'They're a gift, Enda', and kissed me. The next day she asked me to join her on a hiking weekend in Kerry. I was still searching for an answer when I heard myself say, 'Go and fuck yourself, Paddy.'

I missed her for a bit after that; then the word spread that she was in hospital with a nervous breakdown. I tried to lose myself in study, but I couldn't concentrate; it was as if my brain had been invaded by wasps. Some of the class called on Paddy, and I was told she wished me to visit her; I could as soon have signed myself in.

A month later came the bombshell: Paddy was missing; she had last been seen near the canal, in her dressing gown and *slippers. The canal was dragged, the estuary searched, ten miles of seashore combed and combed again. A contingent from the class gave a weekend to the search; I cried off, pleading illness; I was sure I'd be the one to find her. But she was never found. Her two brothers, in Engineering and Science, spent several hours a day for two months searching the foreshore; despite not having done an hour's study, they were given a pass in their exams. Not long ago one of them told me he still looks for Paddy, in trains, in crowds, among down-and-outs on city streets, in parks. It hadn't occurred to me that I wasn't alone in doing that.*

After Paddy's disappearance, the wasps went wild entirely inside my skull. I could concentrate on nothing, I slept little, I feared I was heading for breakdown myself. And then the miracle happened: through Eliot's Four Quartets I encountered your stupendous affirmation: 'And all shall be well, and all shall be well, and all manner of thing shall be well.'

I read it and said it over and over again, at times shedding tears of relief. I saw that it applied to Paddy, alive or dead; I saw that it covered me and everybody and everything, every atom, every stirring of consciousness in the universe, from everlasting to everlasting.

Someone told me that your assertion was not an insight of your own, but a communication from Jesus in a vision. Ironically – since I neither accepted his divinity nor placed much store by visions – this strengthened the attraction of my mantra. I wasn't interested in what he meant exactly, or in what you thought he meant; my faith was not in the speaker but in the words: whatever happens ultimately, on the grandest scale conceivable, will be well; that was enough. I believed, like St Augustine, quia absurdum, out of need. I had found my liferaft. I have clambered on again a few times since.

Would you be good enough to lower your sights for a while and take in a very earthbound story?

I was reared by adoptive parents just outside Sligo. I got on with them as well as, and no better than, other blokes got on with their parents. My father was a vet, and my mother a gardener, but both animals and flowers left me cold. Stones were my thing. I collected them, big and little, for their colours and textures and shapes. We had a cottage beside Ballyloughane strand in Galway, where we spent a month every summer; it was mostly there that I increased my collection. I was eight or nine when that started.

I left school at sixteen and went to work with a stonemason. I loved the hammer and chisel, and I learned fast. Walls we were building, for private houses, but after a year we got a long-term job building an extension to a monastery. I liked the place: the only noise apart from our hammers was the bells, and I always stopped to listen to them. The sound, I thought, was as beautiful as stone, it was a sort of spiritual stone.

But after a year of that, I got restless. I wanted to be a sculptor, but I hadn't a clue how to go about it. I went alone to Galway early that summer to think things over. I brought my tools, and spent a week sitting in front of the cottage, trying to hammer stones into the shapes of heads, a man's and a woman's. I got nowhere, I cried with frustration a few times. I abandoned the work then, and sat staring out to sea or went for walks.

One evening I was sitting on a rock at the foot of a small clay cliff when I had the sense that I was being watched. I looked around and saw a boy sitting in a little cave in the cliff face; he was eight or nine and had the saddest face I'd ever seen. I asked him his name; it was Tony. I asked him what he was doing there and he said he came there most evenings, to think. I asked him a few more things, and he said he didn't want to go home, because his father beat him. His mother was dead. Suddenly I burst into tears, and back in the cottage I cried a long time.

I slept badly, and when I woke, some time before sunrise, there was a little rhyme running in my head:

I'm sitting all alone
And my name is Tony,
And I can't go home
'Cause my father's fist is bony.

I got up, and walked to the cave. I scrambled in and sat there, looking out to sea. As the light grew, there were sounds: a distant car, a boat engine. And then, something else, and I saw a swan flying low over the water. It was in my sight a long time, and, as the beating wings grew fainter, I realized that I was about to go away.

Pulling my bag from under my bed, I pulled with it a sheet of old newspaper. It had a photograph of a man bent over a block of stone with a hammer and chisel. He was a sculptor called Gene Cross and he lived in a place called Pickering, on the edge of the Yorkshire moors. I knew then where I was going. My parents made no objection, in fact they offered me their old car. Two days later I was en route for Rosslare.

The journey was a disaster. I had a puncture, the fan belt broke; I lost hours. I had no map. When darkness fell I was lost in a bog in the midlands. Eventually there was a light, and then a door. The man who let me in was a balding red-haired 40-something with a limp and a mischievous smile. He told me where I was, rustled up a meal and informed me that I was stopping the night. After I'd eaten, he produced a bottle of whiskey and two mugs. I took it fairly easy, but he lashed into it, and talked. About his late wife, his two grown sons, his 500 free-range hens, and the numberless follies of the world. And he laughed, like no-one I've ever heard before or since.

There was light in the sky before the bottle was empty. He remarked that it was St John's Eve, and that led to talk of bonfires and old customs and pishogues. He pointed at a hawthorn tree behind the house; he had no time for yarns about fairies, but he'd be loath to take an axe to it himself, although he'd love to see it gone; the bloody thing was blocking the light and annoyed the shite out of him.

"I'll do it," I said, and he said "I dare you," and two minutes later he was limping towards the tree with me after him carrying a hatchet. He was regaling me with a yarn about a girl who'd stolen his bicycle once after leaving him exhausted in a hayfield, and with the laughter I found it hard to concentrate on my first few strokes. When he reached the crux of his story – how he had stolen a garda's bike to give chase, and got caught – he lost control: whether it was the drink or the limp or the laughing, he staggered, and the axe came down on his head; a jet of blood shot into the hawthorn tree and all over me.

I rushed to the phone, dialled 999 and panted: "Ambulance, quick, for Adam Cockburn, Cappadown."

When I went back to look at him, I was certain that nothing could be done. Then the thought struck me: 'No-one would believe me.' I stripped off, stuffed my clothes in a sack, washed the blood off myself in the bath, and put on a fresh outfit; I threw the sack in the car and hit the road. I was in Rosslare with time to spare for the morning sailing. A few miles out I dropped the sack in the sea; then I puked. When I straightened up there was a woman standing beside me: hippyish, about 50, with long brown hair; she had a glass of wine in one hand, and a wine bottle in the other. She turned the bottle upside down, and a little stream of blood splattered the deck between my shoes.

Then she winked at me and said, "All shall be well, and all shall be well, and all manner of thing shall be well."

She tossed the bottle overboard and walked away.

A couple of days later I was in Pickering, talking to Gene Cross, a giant of a man with grey hair and beard and a warm smile. He was amused at my request to become his pupil, but he said he'd give it a go; I think the fact that Molly, his wife, was Irish, helped. I could earn some money, he said, by building walls in the afternoons; he would give me a few contacts.

In the weeks that followed, I observed Gene working, and performed the exercises he set me. He was doing large pieces in granite, I practised with sandstone and limestone. The first real piece I began to work on was a head. I soon realized it was trying to be Adam's. I became totally absorbed, and missed two afternoons of wall building. When I finished it, I wasn't too pleased, but it was a likeness. Molly's was the next head I tackled, and I was happier with the resemblance; she said I'd made her look like a teenager. (She was 35; she had come to London at seventeen, had met Gene and modelled for him; they had married a few years later and moved to Pickering; they had no family. She ran her own business, a mail order firm selling flower seeds.)

Heads continued to be my thing. I tended towards realism, but always with a hint of caricature – an eyebrow, a cheekbone, a tooth exaggerated. In the course of a year and a half I recreated my teachers and several schoolmates, as well as a number of the townspeople I saw as I went about my work. But sometimes I just doodled with stone, and always found, on recovering my concentration, that I had been working again on Adam's head; on one occasion I had given him the wound of the axe.

I fell in love. With Laura, a young woman who came to give a piano lesson in a house where I was building a wall. I was stunned by her beauty: not so much by this or that feature as by an impression of gentleness, by a radiance. I laid down my hammer and listened to her lesson. And that evening we started going out. I discovered a happiness I'd had no idea of before. We laughed a lot together, yet silence was perhaps our greatest joy.

"Without silence there's no music," she'd say, and she'd tease me about the noisiness of my work. "Ah but look at the results," I'd say, "shapely silence forever."

We kissed with a chaste passion; there was something tentative in both of us, holding us back. I called her my grace note, she called me her wall nut.

Five months and three days after we met, she died: knocked down by a police car while cycling near Selby. I was inconsolable; without Gene and Molly I don't know how I'd have got through. It was months before I could sculpt, and then the only head I wanted to do was Laura's. I did over a dozen versions, trying to catch different expressions. Gene offered to include six pieces in an exhibition he had coming up in York. He even put my name on the programme. It was nice to read 'Gene Cross and Rory Waters', but it was small consolation. Some of my pieces would have sold, but I couldn't part with any of them. A little gallery offered me an exhibition of my own the following year; that helped me to consider new themes.

And then came the next shock: Gene died the following Christmas Day, of a heart attack. Molly insisted that I continue to use his studio, and work hard towards a good exhibition. I began work on Gene's head, but I lost myself and it became Adam's. Molly saw what had happened, and said, "Come with me, I want to show you something." She brought me to the bottom of her garden and pointed to a sculpture under a willow tree: it was a head of Adam which was new to me. "In the weeks after Laura's death", Molly said, "you sleepwalked night after night after night; both Gene and I saw you. You came down here and chiselled this head in the dark. Who is this man?" I told her. Her comment was: "It would have been wiser to stay with the body, but you didn't. Don't torture yourself. It was an accident, and that's what any enquiry would have concluded."

Over the following months we grew quite close. We chatted a lot, observed each other working, went for drives. As exhibition time approached, she helped in all sorts of ways; she was more enthusiastic than myself. The opening was highly successful; I sold several items before the night was out. Molly was ecstatic; she actually began to sing on the way home, and I almost crashed the car with the shock; I'd never heard a note from her before. Back at her house we drank a coffee, and a silence developed. We looked at each other and we knew that something had changed. We kissed, and without a word we moved towards her bedroom. The last thing I saw before she switched out the light was a book lying face down on the floor: *Heart of Darkness*; I thought I'd never read a lovelier title.

In the morning I rose to go to the bathroom. As soon as I stood up, Molly screamed. I turned around; she had the sheets pulled up to her chin and there was terror in her face. She screamed again. "You're my son! My God, you're my son!"

"Are you mad or what?" I asked her.

"Those birthmarks . . . they're my baby's!"

(I have a triangle of little raspberries on my left buttock.)

She told me my date of birth, a thing I'd mentioned to no-one.

I spent half an hour in the shower, scrubbing as if I wanted my skin off. When I returned to her room, Molly wasn't there. I dressed, collected my tools from the studio, scrawled a note saying, *'I'll see you sometime'*, and jumped in the car. I didn't know where I was going, except that it had to be south; *'heart of darkness'* kept ringing in my mind like an alarm.

In a gallery in Chelsea I saw an exhibition of stone sculptures from Zimbabwe. The stone seemed to be alive, and I wanted to be where it was carved. The same day I came across an ad offering a leisurely lift in a jeep to Johannesburg for the price of the diesel. The driver turned out to be a mechanic from Ringsend, and he agreed to take me to Harare. We left on New Year's Day '92 and on Patrick's Day I set foot in Tengenenge, an isolated village in the north-east of Zimbabwe which is home to a community of carvers. It was a weird world to walk into – twenty or so sculptors hammering and polishing outside their houses, their stylized human and animal creations covering acres. I wanted to stay. I found lodgings in the nearby compound, along with dozens of visiting artists and a handful of white writers and academics; I got work on the local farm.

I spent weeks wandering around, watching the sculptors, listening to their explanations about the spirit in the stone, the characters they were setting free, the qualities of steatite, serpentine, springstone, lepidolite . . . I was made welcome by everyone and felt at home. There was one thing, however, that I found disquieting. Every Sunday in the compound the Chewa and Yao people from Malawi would be joined by a few local Shona in the performance of their traditional dances. Masks and animal costumes would be worn, and I could never connect the abandon of these wild creatures with the ordinary individuals who later stepped out of their disguises. I could find no link between what they were and what they were doing, although more than one of them told me they never felt more themselves than in their whirling animal mimicry. I continued to watch every Sunday.

I conceived my own unique project: I would document this community of sculptors, in sculpture; it would be a gift I could leave after me. The artists seemed pleased; they were amused too, much less by my touches of caricature than by my efforts at a realism they found alien. I worked in soapstone, because of its softness, and I could produce a head per week. Over the next two years I sculpted the heads of virtually all those involved in the community: resident artists and their families, visiting artists, academics and the like. There was one man I didn't approach, though: Josia. Josia was an 80-year-old Yao man from Malawi who had recently gone blind, but who continued to sculpt figures based on the masks used in his people's dances: hideous, frightening things. For some reason – and I'm not being facetious – I just couldn't look him in the eye.

One Sunday a Chewa man offered me a mask and costume and invited me to join in the dance. I did, self-consciously at first, but I grew oblivious to everything except the drums and the whirling. I wanted to feel as fierce as I looked. Suddenly I heard myself singing: "Adam was my father! I killed my father!" And I danced more wildly, feeling a new strength and power.

When the dance ended, my new conviction stayed with me, and soon spawned another: Molly was not my mother, she couldn't be, she hadn't recognized Adam's head. On later Sundays when I joined in the dancing, I went straight from killing Adam into Molly's bed.

By May of last year I could have completed my project. But I was flexible: tourists and dealers came to the village and I sold some heads, which had to be replaced; new people came to live in the compound and had to be documented. The work was stretched out until November. Then I set about designing a little gallery, where my collection could be permanently displayed, but almost immediately I fell into a depression. I could hardly get out of bed, I couldn't look at a chisel or a face, I wanted to be dead. No-one could help me. I refused to see any of the local healers.

In January someone said I should talk to Josia; he was a wise man. With the enthusiasm of someone swallowing a toad, I went to his house. He told me to bring him a piece of my work. I went and got a head. He moved his fingers slowly over it and said: "There is no dream here. You must go into the dark and dream, then you must find your dream again in the stone. You came here to run away from your dream. You must make your journey back into the dark, and face your dream, then you will be able to bring the dream out of the stone."

I asked him what I should do with this and the 110 other heads I had stored in an old mining-shed; should I break them, destroy them? In the village, he reminded me, there was a *makuwa*, a cemetery, where, in the early days, unfinished works and pieces judged unworthy to be shown were abandoned; that was where my efforts belonged. I should not destroy them; to leave them as they were, beside the older failures, would be the bravest deed. I did that; I lugged my heads one at a time to the *makuwa*, and left them, any old way, alongside the ancient rejects buried in the grass and weeds. Then I left Tengenenge, quietly, and began hitch-hiking home. The worst of my depression had passed.

I got to London in June. To complete my farewell to Zimbabwe, I revisited the little gallery in Chelsea. To my embarrassment I found a piece of my own on sale – the head of a teenage girl – billed as an example of Shona integrity and imagination. I offered to buy it; the price was that of a second-hand motorbike. I opted for the bike.

Turning up in Sligo after seven years' silence, I gave my mother a shock. My father was two years dead; her flowers were more exuberant than ever; she had been thinking of selling the cottage in Ballyloughane but now that I was home I could have it. I stayed with her for the summer, then travelled to Galway. For three days I sat in the cottage, remembering everything, understanding nothing. And I slept little. Late on the third night I walked the foreshore below the clay cliff; I found the little cave, scrambled in and sat there listening to the waves. After a while I fell asleep. I dreamt that I was making love to Molly; then I was stumbling through a cemetery, tripping over sculpted heads, and pursued by Adam's laughter. The laughter was sinister, and the chase went on and on. I collapsed on a tombstone and read this inscription:

ADAM COCKBURN
LAUGHED HIS LAST
23 JUNE 1988
       ERECT

The bones of two hands protruded through the grass and I heard Adam's voice asking: "My son, my son, why have you forsaken me?" I awoke with my heart pounding.

It was dawn. I staggered from the cave, and was confronted by a sinister black stone which seemed to say: "I am your first self-portrait. Your head is inside me."

I took it up and carried it to the back of the cottage, seized my hammer and chisel, and looked at it for several hours.

I don't know how long I worked on that stone. Yet I did less to it than I had ever done to any other. Realism didn't interest me, what I wanted was to liberate an expression. I often waited hours before striking a blow, afraid of doing damage. Through a long labour I was midwife to myself, and what I eventually delivered was a mouth that fed only on its own vomit and a pair of eyes that looked habitually on horrors. For hair I provided a little interlocking trinity of serpents.

It was dark when I finished, and I fell on my bed and slept till the sun was high. After breakfast I decided it was time to pay my respects. I climbed on my bike and headed east.

In Cappadown cemetery I failed to locate Adam's grave. I decided to enquire among the locals, but first I would have a look around the house.

Not a sign of a hen anywhere. The house looked unlived in; I went round the back. The hawthorn tree was there, the wound at the base healed into a wicked grin. The silence was eerie and I felt cold in the sun. I was approaching one of the windows when the front door opened and Adam emerged, leaning on a stick. Even if he were dumb he'd have spoken first.

"Can I help you?" he asked me, and when I remained stunned he said, "Come in." He put a bottle of whiskey and two mugs on the table.

I refused, spluttering; eventually I said, "I drank out of that mug before."

He didn't know what I was talking about. "Th'oul memory", he commented, "th'oul memory isn't too good. Somethin' happened," he explained, displaying the scar on his skull – a mere four inches of violet. I told him what had happened, and said sorry for leaving the scene.

"I'd have done the same," he said. "And thanks for calling the ambulance."

I told him I thought he was my father.

He laughed, a quieter version of his old laugh. "I couldn't be," he said. "I only ever rode the one woman, and I married her."

"But," I said, "the woman in the hayfield, who stole your bike . . . ?"

"I married her," he answered.

After a while I told him about Molly, how she said she was my mother.

"And if she is itself, sure what harm did you do?" he asked. "You didn't know."

I left the house relieved, and I was half an hour on the road before I realized I was heading for Rosslare.

She was waist-high in flowers when I called; she kissed me on both cheeks. As her face withdrew, I saw myself for an instant in a mirror: she was my mother. Remembering my dancing fantasies, I closed my eyes in shame, but then, for some reason, I smiled.

Over a cup of coffee I told her about Adam, then I asked her, "Who was my father?"

"I have no idea," she answered. "It was rape, by a stranger."

After a silence I said, "Thanks for having me."

"My pleasure," she answered, misunderstanding, and standing up. As I mounted my bike she said, "It's good to know you're there. Give me a shout every few years. And I'll wish you well far away from me."

I called to Laura's grave in Old Malton. For an hour I sat there in the richest silence I have ever tasted, hearing in memory some of Laura's loveliest music. As I left I said my first words, "Laura, be still my grace note."

Back at the cottage, I slept a long time. As I breakfasted I laughed aloud at the melodrama of my self-portrait outside the window. I decided to carve a second face on the back of my head. I began with the eyes: I opened one slightly wide and gave the other the hint of a wink. The mouth was harder. I didn't want the smile too pretentious: a bit of enjoyment, a bit of understanding, that's what I was after, with a suggestion of some hard experience. I managed some of that. For good measure I conferred a little grin on one of the serpents, and I turned another one into a flower.

The sun was coming up as I finished. The tide was out, and a spur of rocks jutting into the sea near the cottage was exposed for a hundred yards. On a whim, I picked up my head and walked out as far as I could go. I wedged the head between two rocks, the smile facing Galway Bay and the stony Burren hills. Then I walked back along the spur, sat on a low rock facing the sea, and closed my eyes.

I got the odd impression that I was being watched. Then I heard the most discreet of splashes. I opened my eyes. I *was* being watched. By a seal, a young female, a few feet away. I couldn't tell what to read into her look, but it seemed almost as human as any human's. Her eyes held mine for maybe a minute, and I couldn't be sure, but I think she may have winked before going down.

That was last Sunday.

Who else could I have sent this to, given the appearance of the hippy woman on the boat? I don't like the story, it is quite alien to my experience. Yes, I admire well-made stone walls, I've read a bit about Zimbabwean sculpture, I dated a music teacher once, but that's about it. Well, there's also this: in his final months my father exasperated me so much that I genuinely, genuinely, wished to split his skull . . . That stuff about the bloke sleeping with his mother, I find that disgusting. The origin of it, I think, is this: on our wedding night – never before – I had the illusion that I was making love not to my wife, but to her mother, who looked just as attractive and only slightly older the one time I laid eyes on her. And that illusion, that hallucination, *has* plagued *me through the dozen years of our marriage: I can never get beyond the opening kiss without finding the mother in my arms; trying to guard against the illusion only brings it on. Zoë hasn't a clue, of course; she likes my passivity, and calls me, as she did the first time, her 'little tie-bye'. Her appetite is voracious: four or five times a week she exhausts me around midnight, often returning to the charge a few hours later before she rises. Pregnancy makes no difference: many's the time I've awoken to find her ballooning and bobbing above me, hurriedly readying me for congress. Do I get pleasure from this? Do I f---! A wonder I haven't become impotent; no such luck. How long, O Lord, how long? I wish I could wish that all will, eventually, be well. Meanwhile, I'll continue taking my tablets.*

Twice in the story, Rory buries his art. I know the source of that. After my parents' deaths I wrote a memoir about my life with them. It was savage, and I found a London publisher without difficulty. I signed the contract one afternoon and walked to the post office. As I brought the envelope to the opening of the post box, a white stick landed gently on my wrist; I looked up, and a blind man said, simply, 'Don't', then disappeared. I withdrew the envelope, walked home, shaking, and put the book in the fire.

Yours gratefully,

Enda Ring.

Postscript

I put the vase
in the middle of the table.
Then I looked at one side
for a while;
then the other side.
Then I walked round it
from left to right;
then I walked back again
from right to left.

Charlie Drage, in
Wolf Mankowitz,

Make me an Offer